GRANMA NINETEEN AND THE SOVIET'S SECRET

Biblioasis International Translation Series
General Editor: Stephen Henighan

I Wrote Stone: The Selected Poetry of Ryszard Kapuściński (Poland)
Translated by Diana Kuprel and Marek Kusiba

Good Morning Comrades by Ondjaki (Angola)
Translated by Stephen Henighan

Kahn & Engelmann by Hans Eichner (Austria-Canada)
Translated by Jean M. Snook

Dance With Snakes by Horacio Castellanos Moya (El Salvador)
Translated by Lee Paula Springer

Black Alley by Mauricio Segura (Quebec)
Translated by Dawn M. Cornelio

The Accident by Mihail Sebastian (Romania)
Translated by Stephen Henighan

Love Poems by Jaime Sabines (Mexico)
Translated by Colin Carberry

The End of the Story by Liliana Heker (Argentina)
Translated by Andrea G. Labinger

The Tuner of Silences by Mia Couto (Mozambique)
Translated by David Brookshaw

For As Far as the Eye Can See by Robert Melançon (Quebec)
Translated by Judith Cowan

Eucalyptus by Mauricio Segura (Quebec)
Translated by Donald Winkler

Granma Nineteen and the Soviet's Secret by Ondjaki (Angola)
Translated by Stephen Henighan

GRANMA NINETEEN AND THE SOVIET'S SECRET

ONDJAKI

TRANSLATED FROM THE PORTUGUESE BY
STEPHEN HENIGHAN

BIBLIOASIS
WINDSOR, ONTARIO

Originally published as *AvóDezanove e o Segredo do Soviético* by Editorial Caminho, Lisbon, 2008.

FIRST EDITION

Ondjaki, 1977-
[AvóDezanove e o segredo do soviético. English]
Granma nineteen and the Soviet's secret / written by Ondjaki ; translated by Stephen Henighan.

(Biblioasis international translation series ; 12)
Translation of: AvóDezanove e o segredo do soviético.
Issued in print and electronic formats.
ISBN 978-1-927428-65-8 (pbk.).--ISBN 978-1-927428-66-5 (epub)

I. Henighan, Stephen, 1960-, translator II. Title. III. Title: AvóDezanove e o segredo do soviético. English. IV. Series: Biblioasis international translation series ; 12

PQ9929.O53A9613 2014 869.3'5 C2013-907298-5
C2013-907299-3

Edited by Daniel Wells
Translation edited by David Brookshaw
Typeset, designed and copy-edited by Kate Hargreaves

Funded by The General Directorate for Book and Libraries / Portugal.

PRINTED AND BOUND IN CANADA

[...]blue because the dusk may later turn blue, pretending to suspend feelings from golden threads, pretending that today childhood is gilded with toy shops[...] —Clarice Lispector

"Blue shouts? Never heard of them."
"They're words shouted on the ocean floor—kids know about them. Birds, too."
"And the fish?"
"Fish still don't know how to shout right. Fish words must be some other colour."
"Have you ever shouted on the ocean floor?"
"Lots of times. You want to try it?"

The explosion woke up even the birds asleep in the trees and the dozy fish in the sea. Colours came out that had never been seen before: yellow mixed with red pretending to be orange in a bluish green, flares that mimicked the strength of the stars reclining in the sky and a warlike rumbling of the kind made by MiG planes. In the end it was a beautiful explosion that lingered in the noises of the pretty colours that our eyes looked upon and never again forgot.

We, the children, stood looking at the illuminated marvels that filled the sky as though all the rainbows in the world had come running to drink a toast on the ceiling of our dark city of Luanda.

An explosion could be so beautiful, and our open mouths attested to a human silence that came from being close to a rumbling sketched on the heights, where that night the birds learned that the world was a very strange place, what with people of so many nationalities, and that in Luanda anything could happen all at once.

It was on Bishop's Beach, in the square with the gas station, close to the entrance of the famous construction site of the Mausoleum.

After looking so long at the colours with their soaring sounds in the lighted-up sky, few people noticed that the enormous construction, which the elders said was vertical, tall and in the shape of a big rocket, this construction of so many dusty tasks and a thousand exhausted workers, had started to no longer exist, leaving behind only an ashen dust that took a long time to filter back down to the earth.

All of this happened very close to the house of my Granma Agnette, better known on Bishop's Beach as Granma Nineteen.

It was in a time the elders call before.

We made drawings in the dirt across from Granma Agnette's house, then fled from the water trucks that came late in the afternoon to settle the dust.

It was a big square with a gas station in the middle that was on a traffic circle so that trucks and cars could loop around it and pretend that they were in a big city.

The Comrade Gas Jockey was able to sleep away most of his working hours because the pump never had any gasoline. He only woke up when he heard the voice of crazy Sea Foam.

"Those stars that fall all of a sudden have names: they're fouling stars and that ain't the weed talking, I know what I says with all these teeth in my mouth..."

On the other side of the gas station was the gigantic construction site of the Mausoleum, a place they were building to hold the body of Comrade President Agostinho Neto, which had spent all these years embalmed by some Soviet experts in the art of keeping a person with an appearance fit to be seen.

Behind the construction site, on the other side of our square where the dust never settled, lay that beautiful thing that taught me about blue every day: the big sea, better known as the ocean.

"You all talk about falling stars, but I know all the dictionaries of the Angolan and Cuban languages. Fouling stars are phenomena of the skies of the dark universe, the cosmic dust and so on... You dipsticks who never went to university schools!"

We, the children, laughed in outbursts so thick we could almost see them sketched in the air. We were struck silent by terror and magic at the words of the comrade lunatic.

"Get this, kids, there are two skies: the blue sky that belongs to our eyes and to the wings of planes and little birds. And then there's a black sky that's as big as a desert."

We were almost not afraid of Sea Foam. He had never done anything bad to anyone.

"Fouling stars melted in the heat of the sun and that's why they fall towards planet world. Our planet is the only one that has water where they can cool down again. They're fouling stars, and one day, after cooling off, I swear, those stars are going to want to return home..."

He shrugged his threads and went off with a nervous laugh that could have been a sob, walking ever faster, raising the dust with his bare feet, going forward as if he were about to enter the sea.

"We're still going to see those stars rise up from the earth to way up there, in the skies that sleep far away dressed in bright brightnesses..."

On our dusty veranda, Granma Catarina, Granma Agnette's sister, would slowly appear dressed in the black of her old mourning garb, with her white hair like downy cotton.

"Still in mourning, Dona Catarina?" asked the neighbour, Dona Libânia.

"As long as the war in our country continues, sister, all the dead are my children."

Granma Nhéte watered the plants, the bushes and the trees with the thin trickle of water that appeared on Tuesdays and Thursdays. She watered the guava tree and the fig tree, the cherimoya tree, the palm tree and the mango tree. Afterwards she soaked the steps and watered the flowerpots.

"Children! Everybody inside. It's snack time."

Snack time was complicated for us: we had to go and wash our armpits, hands and faces before sitting at the table. We ate half a slice of bread, half a banana and a glass of water.

"Anybody who wants to can make *ngonguenha*, but only use a little sugar. It's almost finished."

Sometimes on the way over we grabbed guavas or mangoes that the bats had forgotten to pillage. A little after five o'clock the Soviets' water truck would come by to settle the dust in the street and on the sidewalk.

One of the cousins had the job of listening out for noise. The Comrade Gas Jockey would wake up when the Soviet driver hooked up the water truck on the construction site of the Mausoleum. This was the signal. Crazy Sea Foam would appear at his front gate with a tiny whip that he would bob in the wind around his legs.

"Granma Catarina, is it true that Sea Foam has an alligator hidden in the doghouse in his yard?"

"Maybe," Granma laughed.

"Does an alligator fit in a doghouse?"

"If it's really small."

Some of us were frightened by this tale, others laughed nervously as we ate in a hurry to get out into the street again. Granma Agnette wasn't home. She had gone to a last-minute funeral.

"Here in Luanda people die without giving proper notice. Such bad manners!" Granma Catarina would say.

Swirls of wind lifted the afternoon dust, and the leaves around the Mausoleum square danced in the air without wanting to go very far.

The Comrade Gas Jockey started to close up the gas station, Sea Foam was dancing as though the breeze were a wedding chorus, and many workers, dressed in blue coveralls and yellow construction helmets, were coming out the main gate of the Mausoleum. Men who walked hand-in-hand, laughing, doffing their helmets, drinking a few beers, rubbing their eyes because of the tears conjured up by the dust.

"It must be boring to work," Pi said. "They're all happy when it's time to go home."

His real name was Pinduca, and in the family he was called Pi. Sea Foam, who had studied mathematics in Cuba until he went crazy, told us that Pi was equal to 3.14. Even without understanding, we liked this name that sounded like numbers and had a decimal point.

The work on the Mausoleum was supposed to be almost finished. That tall, ashen part, made out of a cement so hard it would never fall, looked like a rocket and I figure that later they were planning to paint it with the colours of the Angolan flag, though that could have been one of Charlita's lies.

"My dad has a bar where the workers come in for beer. And he hears the comrade workers talking."

"But your dad's bar is always out of beer!" 3.14 teased, and we took off to run through the dust cloud.

The Soviet from the tanker truck honked his horn and spat out his words in the Soviet language, which was really weird and impossible to understand. The Comrade Gas Jockey changed his clothes and his shoes and stood there waiting for the truck to give the whole square a soaking. The workers disappeared and thousands of swallows began to arrive from every corner of the sky. The earth was damp with a beautiful smell that imitated that of real rain when it falls hard to irrigate the world.

The last person to leave the construction site—who wore a different helmet and closed the padlock on the front gate—was the Soviet Comrade Gudafterov, to whom we had given this name because of the way in which he said, almost as though he were speaking Soviet, "Gudafter-noon," even when it was early in the morning or really late at night. We imitated him, then burst out laughing.

"Gudafter-noon, Comrade Gudafterov!"

"Gudafter-noon," he replied in a serious voice.

"Comrade Gudafterov, is it true that the work on the Mausoleum's almost finished?" 3.14 asked.

"*Nyet*!" he said, with the face of a bad guy.

On the other side of the square, the wind was drawing pictures on the sea. Charlita arrived, with her thick glasses.

"Do you see the sun the same as we do, Charlita?"

"Of course."

"And if you take off your glasses?"

"Then I don't see anything. Just stains."

"I'd still like to see those stains some days. They must be like watercolours."

The enormous sun, which seemed so close by, was sinking, as though boiling, into the water of the sea. Maybe that's why here in Luanda the water on the beaches is so warm. And it even seemed that the sun was giving the wind orders to calm down. The wind stopped whistling and all that remained on Bishop's Beach was the wet earth and a silence in which almost nothing could be heard.

"Gran Nhéte is here?" Comrade Gudafterov asked.

"*Nyet*!" I replied.

"Then pleeze say I come back tomorrow."

"Kaput yes," 3.14 invented. "Go ahead, tupariovsky!"

These words came from Senhor Tuarles, who liked saying, "tupariov" for nothing and everything.

Comrade Gudafterov departed, walking with his feet turned in and moving very fast as though he were always late. His car, a Lada Niva of a hideous colour, was on the other side of the street. It took a moment for the engine to catch. Explosions came out of the tailpipe and then he pulled away.

Sea Foam was swirling his whip around. Granma Maria came to tell Charlita to come home. The Comrade Gas Jockey said goodbye and disappeared.

"See you tomorrowov, Comrade!" 3.14 said.

Far away, in the shadowed darkness, the Old Fisherman had just arrived. He got out of his dugout, slowly folded up his net, stowed his two anchors and waved to me.

"Watch out, Elder, the sea is full of salty waters!" Sea Foam shouted. "They're the tears of those who just died."

Very early that morning, someone had heard Comrade Gudafterov utter the word dynamite in his own language. For us, dynamite was a word that came from spaghetti westerns that starred Trinità and fat Bud Spencer, beard and all.

"Maybe you didn't hear right."

"I totally heard right. Dynamite."

"Couldn't you have heard 'Dimitry'? There's another comrade on the construction site with that name."

"I totally heard dynamite. Don't you know that there are some words that are complete internationalists?"

We took a walk past the gasket for the pipes, in which there was a gully full of construction site garbage. Little kids played there with colourful kites.

As we passed Sea Foam's house we heard strange sounds and a heavy chain dragging on the ground.

"That must be Foam's alligator."

"Let's split."

We ran with our arms spread like birds launching into flight. We crossed the garbage dump and went out to the shoreline, hopping between the shattered seashells and clams to avoid cutting our feet.

The Old Fisherman was there sitting next to his dugout, Rainboat. With all the patience in the world, his aged hands undid the nets' difficult knots.

The sea smelled there, but not with that fresh or open smell that came from the scales of fish. It was more a smell of other days, other years, a mixture of seawater and the tar on the bottom of his dugout.

We arrived breathing hard and stood catching our breath while we waited for him to notice us. We buried our toes in the sand and smelled the sea, at last, as a way of smelling the morning.

"I'm not going out to sea today. There's no wind," the Old Fisherman finally said.

"Maybe this afternoon," Charlita said.

"Maybe." His hands continued undoing knots.

"Comrade Fisherman," 3.14 began, "you didn't hear about some explosions?"

"Explosion? How's that?"

"This morning somebody said the Soviets were bringing dynamite to the construction site. Isn't dynamite for making big explosions?"

"I think so." His face took on a worried look.

"In cowboy movies dynamite is for blowing up trains, houses or even caves, to find gold."

"I've never seen a cowboy movie," the Old Fisherman said.

The sea was as flat as a mirror made to reflect clouds and birds. The elders said that the sea was a big mirror for people who tried to fly really high.

"Do birds think, Comrade Fisherman?"

"I don't know if they think, but they feel. They know where they have to go, how to get back, and they never forget the place where they made their nests."

"And do fish think?"

"You'd have to ask the fish that."

"Comrade, doesn't it make you sad to catch so many fish in your net?"

"I catch fish to eat or to sell. The ones I sell give me money for clothes or schoolbooks. I have lots of kids. That's how life is."

"And, Comrade, you never heard anybody say they were going to blow up all of Bishop's Beach?"

The Old Fisherman stopped to look at us with sad eyes. He said nothing. He just breathed: recreating in his chest the coiled sound of the waves. The noise mingled with the flight of birds and the cry of a siren somewhere far off in another neighbourhood.

And the sea awoke, slowly at first, like a newborn swallow, then a little more as it imitated the clouds, until all that we could look at was its dark blue: on the enormous hide of the sea, with Mussulo Island on the other side, a wind came in to push the sun lower to where it sleeps every night.

"Hey, kids, you brought the wind with you."

"We're taking off now. The elders will give us a hard time for being out when it's getting dark so quick."

The square with the gas station was empty. Leaves were being swept across the ground by the squalls. A hot breeze was blowing and crazy Sea Foam was smiling with satisfaction at the gate of his house.

"Anybody who hasn't got an umbrella is going to get soaked. *La lluvia no perdona a los que se ponen por debajo de ella...* Down, dust. Down, evil thoughts! Long live poetry, which can speak of anything!"

Granma Agnette was waiting for me at the gate with her far-seeing gaze. She had seen us run through the garbage dump and had watched us all the way back.

"Get inside. It looks like rain and you're out there running around, just asking for an asthma attack."

The rain fell suddenly, without giving us time to say it was still just starting, with the beautiful odour that washes the dust from the leaves and bothers the bats: on nights like that, they don't fly, the sounds disorient them. Granma Catarina said that since bats only see through their own cries they're like radar, like the MiGs when they make night flights to bombard the japie South African troops.

"Does all that rain fit in the sky, Granma?"

"It's the dead who are crying or laughing. Lots of people are dying out there."

"Don't frighten the children, Catarina," Granma Agnette begged.

"The children aren't afraid of the truth. Rain cleanses the world. I'm going upstairs to close the windows."

I went up with Granma Catarina to witness this ritual. In fact, the windows were always closed, but she opened them really wide, glanced out at Bishop's Beach, or at some neighbour in another house, and pulled the double windows shut with a thump so that nobody could doubt that they had been open. Granma left the room and went downstairs.

I went into the bathroom to close the small window. I stood on the toilet and peeped out at the Mausoleum: in the darkness I saw trucks arriving and lots of boxes being unloaded by military people in those dark green uniforms. I turned out the bathroom light so nobody out there could see me; I'd learned this from a war movie, or someone had told me about it. There were various trucks, many boxes; they put everything in a really big storage shed.

The thunder started, and Granma Agnette's waterworks, too.

"Children, everyone into the bathroom."

The cousins arrived and the bathroom started getting crowded.

The electricity went out, but Granma Catarina had already prepared the oil lamp, with its nauseating smell of slow-burning oil. Granma Agnette said this was the safest place in the house if the roof was struck by lightning. Once we were all in there, it was always the same thing:

"Did you cover the mirrors?"

Granma Catarina laughed, unafraid of the thunder or the lightning. She sent Madalena to fetch the bath towels to cover the biggest mirrors: the display cabinet downstairs in the living room, full of antique dishes and a Chinese tea set, then the mirror in Granma Agnette's room, and a really heavy round one in the hall.

"Girls—Tchissola, Naima," Granma scolded, "take off those bright red blouses right away. Madalena—bring them a change of clothes."

Red, on towels, carpets or even blouses, might attract lightning, and it would be terrible if a lightning bolt hit a person because they said that the bolts came full of totally out-of-control electricity. 3.14 told me once that they should use the rocket of the Mausoleum, in all its height, to catch the bolts and then connect it directly to the poles on Bishop's Beach, and that way we would never run out of light; but they said this wasn't possible and it might ruin the embalmed appearance of Comrade President Agostinho Neto.

Fortunately, Granma Agnette forgot to close the little window and, along with the noise and the lightning flashes, fresh sea air came in and alleviated the atmosphere of so many people exhaling mixed with the body odour of those who had run to get here.

Granma Catarina stayed in her room on the rocking chair, and seemed to be serving herself "a hot drink," which might have been whisky or brandy. Then she lay down for a bit on the floor of her room.

"For those who are already gone and await the others..."

The sea breeze carried a heap of smells that you had to keep your eyes closed to understand, as though it were a carnival of colours: mangoes still green and pretty hanging from the trees, mangoes already gnawed by bats, the green smell of the cherimoya fruit, the dust brushed off the guavas that were about to fall, the smell of Surinam cherries blended with that of the loquat tree, the smells of chicken coops and pigpens, the cries of the parrots and the dogs, two or three bursts from an AK-47, a radio that someone had left on during a news broadcast in an African language, the footfalls of people who were running to get home, or at least to get to a place where they wouldn't get wet, and even if it were already late, the sounds of the bakery that was in the street behind, where they started work so early and worked all night to ensure that the bread arrived hot at the houses of people who spent the whole night sleeping. Which meant that, in the end, the smell of the rain was a difficult thing to describe to someone who wasn't familiar with the bathroom of Granma Agnette's house.

"Are you fallin' asleep, or what?" they asked me.

"Shut your mouth. I'm putting the rain in my thoughts."

"Oh yeah? When you grow up you're gonna end up crazy like Sea Foam. Your thoughts'll be soaked."

"At least I'll know how to speak Spanish."

"You retard. He speaks Cuban!"

A thunder clap like an explosion of dynamite made a blazing light, then burst over us so loudly that we trembled with real fear. Granma Agnette started to pretend that she was praying. Granma Catarina had already told us that Granma Agnette didn't know how to pray; she'd forgotten all the prayers and was reduced to moving her lips, like when we sang a song in English and improvised with syllables that we set to the rhythm of the music.

Granma Agnette grabbed the face towel and covered the small mirror that was above the washstand. I remembered the word dynamite and thought that those trucks might have been from a hidden convoy, that, after all, they didn't want the people of Bishop's Beach to know when they were going to dexplode the houses to enlarge the construction site to complete the Mausoleum.

"Can a lightning bolt ignite a box of dynamite?" I asked an older cousin.

He was really irritated because, at his age, he didn't believe in stories about lightning bolts coming into people's houses in search of big mirrors or children dressed in bright red blouses, yet Granma kept herding everyone together in this spot until the rain passed.

A strong wind extinguished the oil lamp and our eyes took a long time to make sense of the darkness. Then there was a knock on the door downstairs.

"Oh my God." Granma Agnette was afraid.

The girl cousins hugged in a shivering embrace. I was afraid, too, it was just that with my older cousin looking at me, I pretended it was only the cold.

"Who could it be at this time of night?"

"It can only be Father Inácio!" Granma Catarina said.

But though Granma Catarina was joking, it was a serious moment. Nobody wanted to go downstairs and Granma Agnette was kind of a scaredy-cat. She always wanted to send somebody else downstairs.

"Madalena, go see who's there."

"Granma?"

"Granma, what? Don't you understand? Go downstairs and see who's knocking on the door."

There was another knock, this time even louder.

"Death always knocks loudly, that's what I say." Granma Catarina began to laugh.

We all fell into a silence of fear and darkness, relieved only by the light that came in through the small window. We almost didn't all fit into the bathroom, and Granma Agnette started to push Madalena very slowly out the door.

Madalena pushed back and grabbed the door to try to avoid being ejected. It all happened in silence, and it looked like a struggle between two ants.

There was another knock. A thick voice spoke a few words that nobody understood.

"What'd he say?" I asked my cousin.

"He said he's coming to eat you!"

Granma Agnette continued to push Madalena. Since her flip-flops were soaked, she skidded very slowly in the direction of the stairs. Either she decided to walk or she was going to fall down the steps all the way to the bottom.

"Death doesn't like to wait for the rain," Granma Catarina laughed.

The light came back on.

We were all looking at each other, each of us trying to see where the others had finally managed to find a seat. The girl cousins, hugging one another, pretended that they hadn't been afraid. Granma Agnette released Madalena as though she had never pushed her, and the doorbell rang three times.

"You can open the door," Granma Catarina said. "It's just that dumb Soviet!"

It was Comrade Guderafterov's ring, three times as always, with long pauses in between.

"Gran Nhéte, you can oben. It is me, Bilhardov. Very rain here."

"Ten years he's been here and he's never learned Angolan Portuguese. These Soviets are a disgrace to linguistic socialism," Granma Catarina said.

In the time it took him to come in the door, soaking, to squeeze Granma Agnette's hand, we all sat down on the stairs like the audience at a movie matinée.

"Gudafter-noon, kildren."

"Gudafter-noon, Kom-rad," we imitated, and Granma made an ugly face.

Over in Comrade Gudafterov's country it must be really cold because he had the bad habit of always wearing a big, warm coat that magnified his body odour, so that if the wind was blowing in the right direction, people always knew that he was about to arrive.

"Take off that coat, it looks like a bear. All it's missing are claws and a raw fish in its mouth." Granma Catarina was having fun.

Comrade Gudafterov laughed out loud. He looked at Granma Agnette, who didn't know where to look. We weren't going anywhere; we enjoyed these scenes as if they were a live soap opera.

"Gran have hod drink?"

"Tea?" Granma Agnette asked.

"He wants a take-out. Tell him this isn't Senhor Tuarles's bar."

"Saw-ry?"

Comrade Gudafterov's Angolan Portuguese was really very funny, but we'd succeeded in deciphering it. He said "saw-ry" to say "sorry" when he hadn't understood something. "Kildren" was "children," and he always liked to say, "Gudafter-noon"; that was one of his habits. I understand: sometimes a habit is like a torn old nightgown that a person likes because they like it and that they don't want to stop wearing because it reminds them of something nice, or because it soothes their nostalgia for someone who's not there.

"'Saw-ry' is a load of bull!" Granma Catarina said while Granma Agnette went to the kitchen.

The Soviet laughed. There were wrinkles in the corners of his eyes; this comrade must be old. His teeth didn't have a good colour either—only his eyes. All the children knew this: only his eyes were pretty, of a blue that was lighter than that of the sky. We didn't know whether over there in the Soviet Union everybody had eyes like that, or if it was just a family thing.

"Family live in far-away. Bilhardov have sadness." He spoke as though we were all one person capable of conversing with him. "Family big, in cold, in snov. Angol very hod. Gud beer! Very dust."

The cousins laughed and started whispering secrets in each other's ears. Granma Agnette had already said that it was rude to speak in hushed voices in front of strangers, even if they were Soviets. Everybody was distracted, the water was boiling in the kitchen. Poor Comrade Gudafterov! They were only going to give him a cup of tea instead of the vodka he must be nostalgic for. Suddenly I felt bad. I swear I thought about this business of a person mixing different subjects, talking about his family, the "snov," the dust of Bishop's Beach, and his eyes growing shiny, which at times is a warning that tears can suddenly appear. I thought about all of that without telling anyone so they wouldn't give me a hard time. I thought it must all be a sad yearning. Having his whole family living in the far-away couldn't be easy for Comrade Gudafterov. Was that why he always tried to strike up a conversation with Granma Agnette?

Something else that I thought, and which made me want to smile, was that Comrade Gudafterov couldn't even imagine that he was often mentioned in our after-lunch conversations with Granma Agnette.

She did it on purpose to make us take our nap after lunch. There was an instant's chaos. We all went upstairs to Granma Agnette's room, while we listened to the ruckus of Granma Catarina opening and closing windows, murmuring some little prayer in front of the mirror over her dresser, then she drew the curtains to fall asleep and began to snore.

"If you stop hearing me, come and wake me up," Granma Catarina advised. "I'll fall asleep again afterwards."

Granma Agnette hugged each of the many grandchildren as we went into her room. I don't know how we all managed to fit in that bed, even though it was a double; a bed wasn't made to hold so many grandchildren all at once.

She sang the music of slow Fado tunes, adapted to put us to sleep, and nobody slept. She told crazy stories about her friend Carmen Fernández who had become pregnant, but had given birth to a huge bag of ants that bit the inside of her stomach. The second time she got pregnant she finally had a baby, but it had the head and wings of a bird and, as the window was open, it flew away and escaped. Granma said that Carmen Fernández was afraid of becoming pregnant a third time, but even then we didn't fall asleep. Then Granma started with her threats.

"Nobody likes me."

"That's a lie, Granma. We like you."

"Then everyone who likes me is going to fall asleep now."

"No, Granma. We don't want to sleep."

"Then I'm going to accept the Soviet's proposal."

And the joke, which always started as a joke, even though we knew where this story was going, always left someone very sad or even crying.

"The what, Granma?"

"I'm going away to the far-away. The Soviet's already said that he wants to take me to the far-away. And I'm going. No one will regret my absence."

"Granma, don't say that." Someone would start crying.

"Granma's going away to the cold, to stay there with the Soviet's family."

"But Granma, we like to have you here, you can't go to the far-away..."

It was a strange joke, but it worked. In the middle of this conversation we, the grandchildren, became convinced that it was better to sleep a little than to endure the thought of Granma Agnette's departure with the Soviet. It seemed like it took a long time to get over there to the far-away and it must be even more complicated to return from that place whose exact location nobody knew.

"You know verbena leaf?" Granma Agnette appeared with the teacup in her hand.

Comrade Gudafterov made a strange face, sniffed the tea and smiled the way we did when we were asked if the refried beans were good.

"Tankyou!"

Granma Agnette opened the window and saw that all of Bishop's Beach was dark. But we had light.

"These house have electric light! Bilhardov connect to generator for Mausoleum. Gran Nhéte sleep gud. Direct connect to generator. Petromax *nyet*!"

The Soviet lifted the teacup to his mouth but didn't drink. He just laughed, with his mouth and with his blue eyes that looked aquamarine.

"Drink the damned tea." Granma Catarina continued looking at him, as she did with us when she was keeping track of the soup.

"Thank you, Comrade Bilhardov," Granma Agnette said. "And the other houses, can't they also have light from the generator?"

"Other house, other lady. These house very close to Mausoleum. Direct connect."

"Listen here, tupariov, since you're here for tea, which you're not even drinking, just blowing on"—Granma Catarina was like that, she said anything she felt like—"is it true you're going to explode our houses?"

"Dexplode? Nyet. Every booty relocate. New house, pretty. Veranda and all."

"I'm not asking about the veranda. This house has a veranda, too. When it's for?"

"Whan? Month of year?"

"Yes, month of year! And day of month. Whan is the blow-up?"

"No have direct information. Boss General decide. Bilhardov only know Mausoleum."

"But it looks like they already brought the boxes of dynamite, Granma," I said to Granma Catarina.

"Children remain silent and don't interrupt adult conversations," Granma Agnette reprimanded me.

Then, looking as though she were in pain, Granma laid her hand on her leg and rubbed it in the direction of her foot.

"What's wrong, Sis, have you got that old pain?"

"It's been there since the morning, but it's worse now."

"You should call your daughter to find out what can be done. You've been like that for months."

"Pain in food, Dona Nhéte? In Soviet Union doctor resolve problem. Gud doctor."

"We've got doctors here, too. My niece is a doctor, Comrade Bilhardov."

"Then I go sleep. Tomorrov vake up early. Gudafter-noon, kildren!"

"Gudafter-noon, Comrade Gudafterov!" We laughed again.

Granma accompanied Comrade Gudafterov to the gate. We peeped out. They always stopped for a moment to talk at the front gate. Dona Libânia always peeped out of the house next door; whatever happened in our house, Dona Libânia always knew about it, to the point where anybody who had doubts about what had happened or when, could ask Dona Libânia. Even with stuff that happened in other houses that she couldn't see, she always knew.

Afterwards, Granma Agnette came inside, walking with difficulty. She sat down and rubbed her leg again.

"It's a kind of burning."

"Either you phone your daughter or you call the Cuban doctor."

"I'll call tomorrow. It's late now. Children, get ready for bed."

"Anyone who's hungry can have a serving of the soup that Madalena's going to warm up," Granma Catarina said. "Leave it, Sis. Just rest there with your leg stretched out."

The rain had just stopped. A pretty, slow sound, a sort of smothered whistling, became audible in the corner of the yard where the fig tree stood.

We only ate a bite for supper. Nobody much liked the soup, but Granma Catarina stayed right alongside us, watching us with deliberate care.

"It's not the mouth that goes to the food," she taught us. "It's the food that comes all the way to the mouth."

We practised this complicated manoeuvre of eating almost without lowering our necks and still we listened to other rules that we already knew by heart.

"No elbows on the table. The stomach does not lean against the table. We may not have much food, but we know how to eat. And one does not talk with a full mouth, that you know already."

We went upstairs to clean our teeth and pee. Our pyjamas were an old shirt and briefs. It was hot but we had to cover our bodies, even if it was just with a sheet, because of the mosquitoes.

"I don't know why mosquitoes have this vice of drinking blood."

"They must be thirsty."

"Don't talk nonsense."

I squinted out the bathroom window. An owl sat in the highest branches of the fig tree, as though the moon were a little box for keeping photographs and the owl were its own photograph in black and white. A photograph that stirred now and then to utter an owl's cry.

We were still eating breakfast when I heard 3.14 and Charlita shouting outside and calling us by name to go and see what was happening.

It was really early. The sun had already come up, but you could still see that glaring yellow which, in fact, you can't look at. I like the toasted yellow that appears in the late afternoon a lot better, though not during the last few minutes before the sun dives into the sea. Then it's more like a yellow running into an almost scarlet-orange. It's before that. Toasted yellow is a colour that appears very suddenly and disappears too quickly for you to understand that it has passed. But here's a secret: toasted yellow, at times, also appears in my dreams.

"Finish eating first, then you can go out. And I don't want any rushing. Is somebody running after you, children?"

"No, Granma."

"Then eat slowly. You've got the whole day to play. Your lives are just playing."

Adults think our lives are "just playing." It really isn't like that. Charlita's life wasn't always easy, what with the chore of sharing her glasses when the soap opera came on because her sisters also wanted to use the glasses to see clearly; 3.14 had to help at home and with his grandmother's sales work, who travelled far away to sell the bread she had bought cheaply in the bakery on our street; Gadinho's life wasn't always easy either, with having to endure all he couldn't do: he couldn't play, he couldn't have a birthday party, nor were we allowed to give him gifts, nor could he come to our parties, nor, on account of their being Jehovah's Witnesses, did his father accept the gift we all got together to give him. And Paulinho's life, beyond helping at home where he always carted water because most of the time there wasn't any, and with his father always working with heavy pieces of metal because he was a mechanic, he then still had to go to judo practice and get pounded out, because it seems that in judo that's part of practising, and in the first year you only learn how to fall and take a pounding without snivelling in front of the master or your classmates.

"Eat slowly, you've got the whole day to go and play. Madalena, go see if the bakery's opened again."

Madalena Kamussakele would go out and sometimes one of us would accompany her.

That second outing to see if the bakery had already started to sell hot bread was more peaceful. But everyone knew that hours before, maybe even at four-thirty or five in the morning, Madalena had already woken up, and almost without washing her face or cleaning her teeth, with a heap of dreams still in her face and her body, had gone to "put a stone" in the bakery line-up. Since Madalena woke up really early and the bakery was nearby, her stone was almost always at the front of the line.

People did this on Bishop's Beach, and afterwards they were able to go home because sometimes the Comrade Baker was also still sleeping because of his binge the night before, or some funeral that had offered hot drinks, or even because he lacked some ingredient to finish making the bread, maybe coarse salt, or maybe even that there hadn't been any gas in the bread oven's enormous gas canister, and everyone was familiar with the line of stones and respected it. At times the Comrade

Baker himself would open the bakery and await the arrival of the owner of the first stone before he started to sell.

"Nobody moves. This stone belongs to Dona Libânia, it's the greenish stone."

Or then some other kind of tip-off.

"We're going to wait for Madalena from Granma Agnette's house. That tiny little stone is hers."

Rarely did Granma allow us to go with Madalena when it was time to retrieve the stone and actually buy the bread.

I liked the days when crazy Sea Foam was also in the line, wearing his trademark long slacks and shirt of faded cloth, barefoot or in simple, flat flip-flops. He stayed in the line as long as was necessary, in the sun or in the fine rain, with or without dust, whether he was hungry or thirsty, just to be able to approach the Comrade Baker and tell him: "I come only to affirm that I am not yet in possession of the necessary card to usufruct from the renowned services of this hot bakery."

It took me some time to learn by heart this complicated sentence, and even the almost Cuban accent with which he said "hot," prior to withdrawing before the amazement of everyone and the dropped jaw of the Comrade Baker.

"Don't you ever get tired of always saying the same thing?"

"The world has not yet learned the simplest of truths. *La luna* appears every month and we still haven't learned to draw its shape. The more we..."

Sea Foam extended his hand and the Comrade Baker was unable to reject the gesture. He gripped the stamp he used to stamp the bread ration card, and slowly stamped the lunatic's left hand.

"So that no one may say that I did not report for the morning call. Aren't we going to sing the national anthem today, Comrades?"

If everyone remained silent and avoided looking at him, Sea Foam, with the stamp on his left hand and very slowly fanning the whip in his right, withdrew and went to take an early morning swim on the prohibited section of Bishop's

Beach. The Soviet guards, with their skin reddened by the hot sun and their dark blue military uniforms, no longer prevented him from swimming there every morning.

"One day the Mausoleum's gonna fly," Sea Foam kept saying, "and it's gonna take all the blue ants with it..."

In their half-spitting tongue, the Soviets laughed, not understanding even a single internationalist comma or word. They became redder, they adjusted their berets and shook their blue uniforms, laughing at the crazy guy, imitating the herky-jerky gestures with which he sank into the water, without knowing that they were the blue ants and that Sea Foam wanted them to go away on a flight that took off from the Mausoleum construction site.

When Madalena returned from the bakery, she brought the bag of warm bread in one hand and the stone in the other. She hid the stone behind the flowerpot on the veranda, dusted off her hand and left the bread on the table.

"I shall always long for bread. It's hard that coffins are such narrow places."

"Always talking about coffins and death, Catarina. Really!" Granma Agnette didn't like this.

"Death is our next home, Agnette."

Seated on the veranda, I liked to play the game of looking at the white clouds dancing in the sky as the wind pushed them.

In school they taught that the wind was invisible, and in a way it is, but, without wanting to seem crazy like Sea Foam, there are times when I find that, just from how the clouds fly, it almost becomes possible to see where the wind is coming from and, above all, where it's going. If you pay close attention, it's obvious that the wind can't like riding through the sky alone because it always lifts the dust, bends the trees, puffs out the leaves and drags the clouds away. The wind must have a house in the far-away, and it's always trying to carry the clouds home with it. But this is something I keep to myself without telling anyone because other children might call me a nutcase and the elders could want to give me medicine to see whether I'm all right in my head.

When I had my eyes closed, I played another game. It was called "Guessing noises" and it was nothing more than this: keeping my eyes closed and listening to the tiny noises in Granma Agnette's garden. The steps of Granma Maria, who was Charlita's granma, in the yard next door, the scuffing of her sandals and the momentum of her body could tell me whether or not she had the bowl of *kitaba* on her head. The clinking of the keys that hung from Comrade Gudafterov's belt could tell me whether he was going to drive a tractor, open the large front gate or go to the pantry where he had hidden a bottle of vodka. The sound of Granma Catarina's shoes let me know how many steps she had climbed on her way to the window the first time she did this in the morning—"I'm going to see if I left the window open"—at an hour when she still had the strength to go upstairs quickly; a different sound could mean that she had turned left and entered the bathroom. The wet sound of a watery rag being swirled around meant that Granma Agnette had already tidied up the kitchen and Madalena was on her knees cleaning the floor, which she did before going outside to shake out the carpets and give corn to the chickens; or, if there was no corn, it might be leftover dried breadcrumbs. Later she might sweep the yard of the leaves that fell from the fig tree, and only at the end would she clean the parrots' cage in a strange manner, for when Madalena Kamussekele was near, the parrots stayed peaceful and refrained from speaking nonsense. The last of the noises, the one, to tell the truth, I liked best, was the most attractive and most difficult of them all: to stay very silent, to try to breathe slowly with my eyes completely closed, in order to listen, through the tiny openings in the low wall, to the sound of the slugs that sat on the stones in the garden or climbed the large leaves that looked like enormous highways for slugs to scale.

"How many slugs?" Madalena knew my game. "Without opening your eyes, you cheater."

"I don't need to cheat."

"How many?"

"Three."

"You're wrong! There are four of them."

"It can't be!"

But it was. A smaller one on the tip of the leaf and lacking the slightest trail of drool had made me get the number wrong.

"It doesn't count, the little one didn't move. There's no way I could know."

"It doesn't matter. You're wrong." Madalena went happily back to the yard.

3.14 was at the front gate, laughing at our craziness.

"What are you guys doin'?"

"Nothing."

"Nothing? It's 'nothing' when the two of you talk about a bunch of slugs climbing up a leaf?"

"Hey! Don't shoot your mouth off. What's happening?"

"What's happening is that your Granma's house has tons of light and we're stuck and can't even watch the soap opera. They're sayin' your Granma's got pull with the Soviet tupariov. Maybe they're even lovebirds."

"Stop that. I'm gonna smash your face in!"

"Cool it, it's just stuff I heard. But you guys had light yesterday, that part's true."

"I'd like to talk to you about that."

"Are we gonna connect a cable from your Granma's house? That would be awesome."

"No. We're going to cut the cable."

"What do you mean?"

"If the other houses don't have light, the best thing is not to have it. It's just gonna cause a scrap. On top of that, the TV's on the blink and it's useless for watching soap operas. Do you know which cable it is?"

"I know. Aren't you gonna catch hell from your Granma?"

"Only if she finds out. Are you a little tattletale like Charlita? Eh?"

This was the best way to do it. 3.14 hated being called a tattletale, or being compared to girls.

"We just need a pair of wire cutters."

"I think Madalena could help us."

"Is she gonna ask for something?"

"Like what?"

"Like something in exchange for the wire cutters."

"Let's go find out."

In the yard the parrots were whistling or speaking nonsense words that Granma didn't like at all. They could utter combinations of nonsense, some Angolan sentences mixed with Russian, and even a few words of Cuban. For example, they said, "*cabrón,*" a lot, "*que te parió,*" or another phrase that they had learned from the movies—I think it was pronounced "fak iu"—which you couldn't even repeat.

One parrot, the one with very light ash-coloured feathers, was called Just Parrot, and the other one was called His Name, as a result of a tale that isn't worth telling right now. This His Name was an old parrot whose age nobody knew. His wings had been clipped and his whole body singed, and he was brought to our yard by André, a commando who had picked up the parrot after some nerve-wracking battles south of Kwanza-Sul Province.

"A parrot all burned like that?" Granma Nhé laughed. "Are you sure he's alive?"

"Yeah, Granma."

"Look here, I don't want any bewitched animals here in the yard. What's his name?"

"It's His Name."

"How do you know?"

"That's the name we gave him. The soldier who found him had that name, too."

"And where is that soldier?"

"He died in the explosion that the parrot escaped from."

His Name ate with enthusiasm. It must be because the war, since it makes you afraid, stimulates your appetite. When he arrived, for the first few days, Just Parrot started getting thin like he was almost finished. Later we had to give them food in separate cages because His Name ate with an appetite from the old days.

"What are you guys doin'?" Madalena met us near the big cage.

"I was remembering the tale of His Name. Is it true he came right out of an explosion that didn't kill him?"

"Those are André's lies."

"The commando's lying, Madalena? Don't shoot your mouth off, or André's gonna give you a beating that'll last till midnight."

"He's gonna give it to me right now? At least I'll put up a fight…"

"Haha! You're gonna fight with the commando? Not even a regular soldier."

"Hush, keep it down, the hens are layin' eggs. What did you come here to do?"

"We need a pair of wire cutters."

"Wire cutters? What for?"

"We can't say."

"Then I can't help you."

"But do you have them or don't you?"

"I *can* have them."

"Madalena, in that case we don't even know if it's worth telling you. Because if you don't have them, then you're going to squeal on us and we'll be stuck without the wire cutters."

All this conversation confused her. That was actually our objective: to start blabbing until she said whether or not she had a pair of wire cutters and what she was going to ask for to lend them to us without anybody finding out.

Madalena kept tabs on a whole bunch of keys. She could get into the animals' hutches, open the parrots' cage, the doors of the house, the pantry, and even the big garage door, behind which were a thousand objects covered with dust that made asthmatic people cough.

"You guys...You talk and talk and you don't say anything."
"You're the one who's not replying."
"What was the question?"
"The question was about the wire cutters."
"There must be a pair in the toolbox."
"You can't just lend them to us?"
"'Just lend them'? Just how?"
"Just like that."
"And if they catch me in Granma's stuff? Aren't they 'just' going to give me a thrashing?"
"No, Granma will only give you a kind of thrashing."
"I can go see if they're there."
"Thank you, Madalena."
"What's this thank you stuff? Thank you is what you say to the Comrade Teacher in school. Here there's going to have to be salt for us to eat with green mangoes."
"But haven't you got the key to the pantry?"
"No. It's in the display cabinet."
"And the key to the display cabinet?"
"It's in Granma's room."

It was agreed: we would get her salt in exchange for the wire cutters. Later she showed us a huge pair of wire cutters with a plastic grip that would be great for cutting an electric cable. We had already seen this in movies, and everybody knew that to cut an electric cable you had to be wearing shoes, wrap the wire cutters in a piece of cloth and not have wet hands or feet. If the wire cutters had a plastic grip, that was even better. In any event, we flipped a coin to see who would actually go and cut the cable and who would guard the entrances in case some elder, or even Comrade Gudafterov, appeared.

"Good, if something happens, you know what to do, just give me a kick," 3.14 requested. "If you don't, we could both get stuck here by the force of the electricity."

The cable was behind Granma Agnette's house. We dug down a little and found it. Even though Comrade Gudafterov had buried it so that no one would see it, 3.14 is good at finding those things. We followed the wire for a bit and soon understood that this had to be the one.

"Do I cut it?"

"Affirmative, Comrade."

At first it was difficult, then we decided that the two of us would have to push down together.

We heard a noise from the side of the Mausoleum construction site and hid behind a really dusty avocado tree that was breaking the houses' foundations with its roots. It was Comrade Dimitry going into a shed with cages full of brightly coloured birds, more than one of which had parrots inside. Maybe it was the same place where the boxes of dynamite were hidden.

3.14 picked up a rock and threw it in the direction of the cages. I had to grab him and drag him back to our hiding place. Comrade Dimitry dropped a cage containing some parrots, which started shouting, "A single people, a single nation!" and "National Radio, broadcasting from Luanda, capital of the People's Republic of Angola," with a voice just like that of the comrade on the radio who said those words on the news every day at one PM and eight PM.

We smothered our laughter so that we wouldn't be caught.

"Let's split now."

We took advantage of Comrade Dimitry's confusion and fled.

We ran into the yard to return the wire cutters to Madalena before anyone could arrive and make her feel like telling on us.

"Here they are, Madalena. Thanks a lot."

"What kind of thanks is that? I already said: coarse salt after lunch, because at the end of the day they're going to bring green mangoes."

"Sure. We'll bring it later. Nobody came by?"

"No. They've got company."

"Who is it?"

"The neighbour. Dona Libânia."

"Then it's just a visitor."

"No, because Dona Libânia is talking as if she was three visitors. And she eats more peanuts than the parrots."

"Madalena...Do you know if the light went out in the house?"

Madalena didn't reply, and as everybody was sitting in the living room looking at Granma Agnette's extended leg, we took advantage of the situation to go to the pantry to swipe the coarse salt.

"You go by yourself. It's only a little salt, your hand's big enough."

"You're afraid of getting caught."

"It's not that, it's just that in my house they already thrash me all the time, and if we get caught here I'm gonna get it again for something that's not even my business. I already helped you get the wire cutters and showed you where the Soviet's cable was."

"Okay, I get it. So cover my back."

"And if somebody comes?"

"You make the noise of that drunken cat."

"What cat?"

"The one on the Cambalacho soap opera. Haven't you seen it?"

"No."

"Hey, that means we don't have a communication code in case of an emergency."

"In the time we've stood here talking you could've already swiped the salt."

He watched the living room and it went really fast. A handful of salt would be enough. I ran out into the yard to call Madalena.

"Madalena! Take your salt."

"Hey, is that how you hand it over? Without wrapping paper or anything?"

"Whoah, are you jokin'? You think this is the people's store, or what? Here it is, if you want it."

We were on our way out through the yard, but they heard our footsteps.

"Children!" Granma Agnette called. "Come and say hello to everyone."

"We can't, Granma. We're really sweaty."

"I said come inside."

Still holding our breath, we entered the living room. I cleaned my hands in my pockets to avoid showing any sign or smell of salt.

"Take your hands out of your pockets. What kind of bad manners is that?"

"Sorry, Granma."

"Say good afternoon to Dona Libânia, who came to visit Granma."

"Good afternoon, Dona Libânia," I started.

"Who came to visit Granma," 3.14 concluded, and the elders laughed. I don't know why.

But it helped. Dona Libânia herself said, "Go play, you little rascals." Granma Nhé made a sign with her eyes that we could go outside.

"May we be excused, Granma?"

"You can go."

When we got to the wall of Senhor Tuarles's house, his daughters weren't there to come and play with us. At the big gate made out of metal grillwork that barely existed any more, on a tiny, pretty little bench, Granma Maria was sitting selling *kitaba*.

"Good afternoon, Granma Maria." We greeted her and left at a run, hitting the sand hard with our feet to raise the dust and imitate the cars when they skidded from driving too fast, and with our mouths we made the noises of acceleration and locked wheels, changes of speed and skidding as well.

"Stop! Good morning, Comrades! Complete vehicle documentation, please, and personal documentation for the respective comrades!" crazy Sea Foam said, very close to us.

"Comrade Agent, these vehicles belong to our bosses, we're just the drivers." I joined in his joke; 3.14 was afraid of Sea Foam.

"These vehicles are clapped out, with loud exhaust-pipes?"

"Yes."

"Accelerate for a moment so that I can test the level."

"Vrummm! Vrummm!"

"It's within the limit. Who are your bosses?"

"They're comrade bigshots, minister types."

"Then you can go ahead. And careful with the maximum speed and sliding on slippery curves. *¡Buena suerte!*"

"Yes, Comrade. Thank you and until tomorrow."

"*Hasta mañana.*"

We continued saying "Vrummm" with our mouths; we accelerated like hell and lifted a lot of dust until we stopped, tired out, on the other side of the square to rest our bodies, in search of shade that wasn't there. The Comrade Gas Jockey looked at us and laughed.

"Run out of gas?"

"Yes."

"You can come and stock up."

We walked over really slowly, with the sweat dripping from our soaking chins and armpits. I stopped suddenly.

"Come on," 3.14 called to me.

"You've got to push, buddy. I ran right out of gas. We're going to have to bleed the gas-line."

"I caught you in a big fat lie. Bleeding is for gas-oil cars."

"Hey, that's right!"

We leaned against the gas pump. The Comrade Gas Jockey had a bottle of water. First he dampened our hands so that we could wash our faces and then he gave each of us a mouthful to drink.

"Some day," he gripped the lever for putting gas into the cars, "you could even drink right from here."

"Why, Comrade?"

"Because the bottom of this gas pump collects water. All it's missing is little fish. The pump must have a puncture. Some day I'll bring a fishing rod to work."

"That would be really cool."

"Shush! It's a secret, the boss can't know, or the Soviets. The blue ants are real tattletales."

"That's right."

We saw a white Lada coming down the long street of Bishop's Beach. It was coming from the Blue District.

"You know that car? Somebody's ill."

"Who does it belong to?"

"It belongs to the Comrade Cuban Doctor, Rafael KnockKnock."

"Rafael what?"

"You guys'll understand." The Comrade Gas Jockey stood there laughing to himself.

The Lada made a circuit of the square and stopped right in front of us.

"*Buenas*, Comrades!"

"*Buenas tardes.*" Maybe the Comrade Gas Jockey spoke Cuban, too.

"Hello, children. *¿Cómo están*?"

"Frigging tupariov!" 3.14 didn't like to be called a child.

"Take it easy, 3.14. Are you being rude to a doctor you don't even know?"

He calmed down. "*Buenas*, Comrade Doctor."

"*¿Dónde está* Comrade Agnette's house?"

"She's my Granma."

"*Muy bien*. Can the *compañero* fill it up, *por favor*? I'm going to make *una visita*."

"*No puedo, no.*" The Gas Jockey started to laugh. "Because that car of yours runs on gasoline."

"*Sí*, of course, *hombre*."

"Yes, but of course, I only sell salty water with a few gas fumes."

"Really?" The doctor was aghast.

"I'm only telling you true truths. Go make your house call, I'll watch your car."

"*Gracias*." Then he spoke to me. "Will you come with me?"

"*Sí*. What's your name?" I tried to improvise in Cuban. 3.14 laughed.

"*Me llamo Rafael*. But they call me KnockKnock."

"Comrade Rafael, here in Luanda we don't like ugly names, and the comrade might become a victim of somebody violently taking the piss out of you. Just don't say I didn't warn you."

"Even though I don't understand you well, *te lo agradezco*."

"Let's go. My Granma's foot is hurting."

"The left foot?"

"Of course, Comrade. Of course."

After climbing the three steps where I liked to sit, we reached the door. The Comrade Cuban Doctor looked at me with eyes that gleamed as though he were a child younger than I. He gestured like someone who was about to perform some sort of magic. He bent down a little, switched the case he was carrying to his left hand and with his right hand knocked very slowly on the door, so gently that he seemed to be caressing the old wood of Granma Agnette's house. He spoke in a low voice.

"Knock-knock. Ha-ha-ha!"

That chuckle ruined the mood and, to tell the truth, I didn't even understand what it was all about.

"*Un ritual,* little *hombre*, only *un ritual*," he said, before knocking loudly on the door.

Madalena opened the door, her smile full of teeth.

"*Buenas. La señora Agnette, por favor*?"

"Come in, Comrade."

Granma was about to get up, but the doctor said it wasn't necessary. I looked at the floor to see if there was something blocking her path or if the surface was wet. Nothing.

Before taking another step, the Comrade Cuban Doctor looked with a smile at Granma Agnette, looked around the whole living room, saw the black-and-white television with the blue plastic over the screen, looked at the display cabinet and the chairs in the dining room, saw the photograph of Granpa Mbinha on the wall and in that moment the old clock hanging close to the stairs gave the muted sound of its bells striking the hour. All he didn't see was Granma Catarina, who was in a corner, dressed in black and regarding us in silence.

"Don't let poverty bother you, doctor. This is a simple home," Granma Agnette said.

"May I?"

"Yes, of course. Make yourself at home. Please be seated."

Granma Catarina went slowly up the stairs but did not utter her usual phrase, "I'm going upstairs to close the windows," and no one seemed to be looking at her. Madalena went to the kitchen and returned with a tray on which there was a glass of water.

"Would you like some cold water?"

"*Sí. Gracias.*"

They talked about sore legs and other doctor stuff. Granma explained that the pain was getting worse and that she could barely feel the tip of her left foot.

"Problems of *circulación*. Age, *señora*. Age does not forgive."

Granma smiled that hesitant smile of hers, of somebody who may not understand.

"Your daughter, *la doctora* Víctoria, asked me to come and see you. May I touch your leg?"

"Yes."

Granma Catarina did not come downstairs. Since Madalena was keeping Granma Agnette company, I went slowly upstairs as well.

The bathroom window was open and I felt a tiny breeze of the sort that the elders say gives you a cough and that can also be called a "whiff." I liked that word "whiff" a lot. Later I also learned that a room where the windows had been open for a long time could be said to have been "aired out."

"Except that you have to be careful, Granma."

"Why?"

"Because it can also be said to be 'mosquitoed out.'"

Granma Catarina laughed at the words I invented during our conversations.

I opened the door to her room. Her rocking chair bobbed slowly with the black shawl draped over the armrests.

"It's time to close the windows." Her very low voice frightened me.

“You gave me a start, Granma Catarina.”

“Sorry, son.”

“Granma, aren’t you going downstairs to hear the Cuban conversations of Comrade Doctor KnockKnock?”

“I don’t like to appear in front of strangers, my dear.” Granma Catarina’s voice was sad. She closed the windows of the room, which was very dark. “Go downstairs, my dear. They might need you to understand the Cuban language.”

“You’re staying here all by yourself, Granma, without any light?”

“I’m not afraid of the dark any more.”

Many years had passed since the Soviets had ceased to prohibit Sea Foam's swims on the prohibited beach, and the fishermen who had already been living there so many years before—before the Soviets, even before present-day Angolans and before the Portuguese—were also allowed to enter and leave as they wished without anyone telling them that beach was "closed to the public."

We, the children of Bishop's Beach, normally went on undercover missions to spy or to swim.

Madalena, though Granma Agnette never knew about it, also went there from time to time to go swimming with her boyfriends, and stayed in the water for a long time doing I-don't-know-what, even if the water was cold or the sea was rough.

"When she shows up with a belly, everybody's going to say it was the sea that did it," the Old Fisherman used to say.

One day we went there early in the morning.

3.14 came to call me to run and see the sea with him. Thinking our mission was to dive in search of pretty seashells and conches, I started to look for my swimsuit.

"You don't need it, just come. We're not going to dive. This is a spying mission."

At that hour Madalena still would have been in the bread line-up or even, if it were a fishing day, waiting for a shipment that might come in only after ten o'clock.

"Just come. I'm going to show you something."

I didn't hear voices in the house. Granma Agnette must have gone out with someone. I called twice more, but Granma Catarina didn't answer. Maybe it was too early for her to appear.

The Luanda sun starts to get hot very early, and it usually comes up before six in the morning. Half an hour later, it's already hot enough to burn skin; the body discreetly begins to sweat, and when the Soviets laugh they turn red like lobsters emerging from boiling salted water. That's how they prepare lobsters: I've seen it at Aunt Rosa's house. They boil the stupid lobsters, they put in coarse salt and, before serving them, Aunt Rosa makes a sauce of lemon, hot spices and a little more salt; she also puts in olive oil or even, if Uncle Chico asks for it, sugar-cane rum.

"The Soviets are strange people," Granma Catarina used to say. "They catch the sun but they don't like to swim."

The Soviets wear blue uniforms of heavy fabric that's good for making rags for wiping the floor, so Madalena told me, a fabric that's absorbent and dries quickly in the sun; it's true, it makes wiping-up cloths that last a long time or even, if properly cut and stitched, good doormats for the kitchen. The Soviets from the Mausoleum construction site never let go of their AK-47s and only when it's very hot do they take off their uniform tops. That's when we see just how strange those blue lobsters are: underneath, they still have that tight green shirt that soldiers like to wear. They patrol the construction site and the beach, but, even when it's hot, I figure they can't have authorization to dive in because they stand close to the water, they chat with the fishermen, at times they make fun of Sea Foam and laugh at him, but they don't go in.

"The place for lobsters is in the sea, *compañero*," Foam tells them, but they don't lift a finger. They break off to speak, spitting Soviet, and they also like to spit on the ground.

"*Oye*, that smell *se llama* B.O.!"

We laughed at the Cuban spoken by Sea Foam, his clothes soaked as he came out of the water, with his Rasta dreadlocks full of sand and trapped, glinting seashells.

Foam's swims took place early in the morning, sun or no sun, whether in spots of rain or a downpour, with thunder or grey clouds, with or without medusas in the water.

"My body's dirty, but *mi alma,* my soul, is clean... Not everybody can say that, right, little lobsters?" The Soviets looked away, shielding their eyes from the sun and not allowing the children to see their broiled faces. "The elders say: when one is not *bienvenido*, one must leave...Hahaha!"

At times he took off his clothes. Underneath, Sea Foam wore outfits so old and dirty it was impossible to tell what fabrics they were made from. At other times he went in with his clothes hanging on his body, and not just a few of them; when he came out of the water, they must have weighed a ton.

He wobbled, laughed as he started running and laughed even more if we were there. He knew that we watched his every move attentively and that later we'd go tell the others. He wobbled, ran as though he were one of those people who know how to dive into swimming pools, like athletes at the Olympic games who dive in fast without making the water stir, except that Foam would suddenly seize up and enter the water almost in slow motion. It was really funny, he seemed to be saying excuse me to the fish and the seashells; he sat down right on the shore and let his body sink into the waves where there wasn't enough water for even a baby to go under.

"I don't have a bath at home, but they can't say I never took a foam bath."

That was how he got his name, Sea Foam, there on the shoreline of Bishop's Beach, where there was a huge blotch of white foam deposited by the breaking waves to ensure that the water merely lapped against the sand. Only if you walked far out did you lose your footing. There the foam disappeared, but closer in, where we also liked to pick up pretty seashells, it was just clean white foam, completely white as you looked to the right and the left, with Sea Foam's body making a dark stain in the whiteness.

"*Oye, niños, es el cabello del mar*... The hair of the sea, do you understand? I mean, hahaha..." He went under for a second, dipped all of his hair in the foam awash with sand and shattered seashells, came up almost breathless and then puffed like a little whale. "I mean... I'm just a louse in the white hair of the sea."

3.14 looked at me with an expression of pity. Lots of people on Bishop's Beach pitied Sea Foam. I never really understood this: Why pity him? A person who went swimming every day and laughed and said that there was the white hair of the sea; a person who spoke Cuban and knew the stars in the sky and the mathematical value of Pi and—who knew for sure?—a person who kept an alligator in a doghouse; maybe even a person who was happy, and only he could know this. 3.14 put his finger to his head to signal that Foam was cuckoo, demented, crazy, but to tell the truth I don't know if Foam was crazy like those real crazies people talk about.

"Maybe he's just a different kind of person," as Granma Catarina said. "You kids have to show respect."

I loved Sea Foam's swims in the white foam.

"Let's split, this is taking too long. We've got other business to settle."

3.14 had those phrases of his: "other business to settle." I figure he liked to imitate how the elders talked, and he also learned by heart lines from soap operas, even soap operas he had never seen: words spoken by Senhor Nacib in some episode of *Gabriela* or something, or some comrade politician someplace in the arsehole of the world in the Brazilian backlands, I think it was called Sucupira and he was something like Odorico Paranguaçu.

"It's not 'Paranguaçu,'" he corrected me, "it's 'Paraguaçu,' and he's one hilarious comrade."

"But you haven't even seen those soap operas, 3.14. Excuse me, but you can't know."

"You bet I know because people tell me about them. I know tons of lines from tons of soap operas my aunts saw when we weren't even born."

"But your aunts didn't even have television. They were off in the bush with the guerrillas, shooing the mosquitoes off their legs." I was giving him a ribbing.

"You're full of it...In the bush they have medicines and plants that keep away the mosquitoes."

"Just listen"—he didn't like me to talk about this—"in the bush did they have paper to wipe their tails?"

"And in your Granma's house, when you don't have toilet paper, how do you clean up?"

"We've got newspaper pages...You just crumple them up a bit and they feel smooth."

"Then in the bush they had leaves...You think being a guerrilla was a joke?" He got nervous when we took the piss out of the guerrillas.

"Cool it, I'm not talkin' about the guerrillas. I'm just sayin' that sometimes you must make up a few lines from those soap operas you haven't even seen..."

"I'm not in the habit of making things up. It's just that sometimes it's necessary to do a bit of adapting."

"What do you mean by 'adapting'?"

"Like you mess around with things a bit...The story gets better and the person who's listening enjoys it more."

"I guess my grandmothers do a lot of adapting."

"I guess so. Let's get going."

We came across Charlita with a piece of paper in her hand and a worried look on her face. She was sweating in the sun and her super ugly glasses were sliding off her nose.

"Hey, how come you don't use one of those little straps to keep your glasses in place?"

"Straps are for Sea Foam's alligator. If you like him so much, why don't you use a strap?"

"Jeeze, you don't have to talk like that."

"How's it going? Do we have results, Comrade?" There

was 3.14 with that elder-talk.

"The results are tons of houses."

"What are you guys talkin' about?"

"Charlita's discovered the mark they invented."

"What mark?"

"For the houses that are going to be dexploded."

"Isn't it 'exploded'?"

"I prefer 'dexploded.' Isn't Sea Foam speaking Cuban all the time? Then I can speak Angolan here on Bishop's Beach. Comrade Charlita, what's the latest on the situation?"

"Lots of houses are marked. They mark them at the back, on the wall that faces the alley. They use a Soviet letter."

"And the houses that don't have a side facing the alley?"

"They mark the sidewalk. A little ways away."

"Is your place marked, Charlita?"

"Yeah."

"And my grandmother's house?"

"That too. They even marked the gas station, the bakery and the Kinanga Cinema. Bishop's Beach is gonna practically disappear."

I felt a teary sadness rising into my eyes and had to pretend it was the sun. 3.14 also looked strange as he surveyed many of those houses of our neighbourhood of dust and children's games. A huge tractor passed by very close to us. It was heavy and made a lot of noise but nobody got out of the way. The driver swore under his breath, the main gate of the Mausoleum opened and the tractor went inside. Then there was an odd silence.

"Good morning, Pioneers." It was the Comrade Gas Jockey. "You have to leave now. I'm going to hose down the station."

Half-smiling, we walked slowly in the direction of the house of Charlita's father, Senhor Tuarles. The Comrade Gas Jockey did that almost every morning. He hefted his broom, put on rubber boots, unrolled a hose, turned on the faucet and there was no water.

"How strange, there's no water in the faucet." And he would put everything away again, very slowly.

What was strange were elders who did things over again every day in spite of knowing that nothing changes. How many years had it been since there had been water at that gas station?

We sat down on the sidewalk, between Granma Agnette's house and that of Senhor Tuarles. A mark in pale ink was there, right on the edge of the potholed sidewalk.

"That's the mark."

"But you don't even speak Soviet. How do you know that says they're going to dexplode?"

"Cause yesterday morning in the middle of the night I saw a Soviet make that mark."

"In the middle of the night? You were awake?"

"Not me. It was my Granma Maria."

"Granma Maria was awake in the middle of the night? Then how is it that she gets up early in the morning to make her *kitaba*?"

"Granma Maria doesn't need to wake up early because she doesn't sleep."

3.14 gave a doubtful look, but I believed Charlita. Every morning Granma Nhé says that she hasn't slept even though I hear her snoring at night when I go to pee in the dark. But, for example, Granma Catarina doesn't sleep at all. Either she sits in the rocking chair in her room, or she goes to the kitchen, or I hear the sound she makes when she goes up and down the stairs, but she doesn't sleep. Or maybe she sleeps in the morning, but it's unusual to find Granma Catarina moving around the house before noon. And if she moves around, she doesn't speak.

"All that's left for us to find out is when they're going to do this."

"I figure they won't give us any warning." Charlita spoke in a sad voice. "Because if they warn us, it's going to cause an uproar. The day they dexplode is the day they'll arrive with news of new houses, in a neighbourhood nobody's ever seen."

"If that neighbourhood doesn't have the sea, what's the Old Fisherman going to do?"

"And what about Sea Foam? Where's he going to swim?"

"You guys aren't seein' the whole problem we got with this." 3.14's voice had become serious. "The problem is that there aren't even any houses in that neighbourhood."

"What do you mean?"

"Is it possible that neighbourhood exists?"

"It must exist, 3.14. Comrade Gudafterov says..."

"Comrade Gudafterov has a house in the far-away. This here is just a borrowed place for him. He can tell us whatever he wants."

"But they're always talkin' about that new neighbourhood. It must exist."

"And peace exists?"

"Huh?"

"Well, they're always talkin' about peace, but as far as I know it still doesn't exist. Ask your Granma Catarina, who talks with the dead..."

"I don't like conversations about the dead early in the morning," Charlita begged.

"That's why I'm saying this." 3.14 looked in the direction of the Mausoleum construction site. He closed his hands into improvised binoculars with little holes to see in the distance. "First we have to remove the marks... But the most important thing..."

"Go ahead."

"Only if nobody squeals."

"Go ahead then."

"We have to dexplode the dynamite."

We heard the sound of the Comrade Doctor Rafael KnockKnock's white Lada turning into the square. It stopped right in front of us.

"*Buenas*, Comrades!"

"*Buenas*," we answered in unison.

"Is your *abuela* here?"

"*Sí.*"

"Come with me."

I winked at the others to indicate that we would continue our plan later and they made a signal that they had understood.

"You must have courage, *compañero*."

"Why?"

"Your *abuela* is not well."

"What's wrong with her?"

"A serious *problema*. We are going to talk with her."

"More serious problems! Jeeze!"

When we reached the veranda, the living-room door was slightly ajar, but Comrade Rafael didn't knock firmly. He closed the door in order to be able to knock gently.

"KnockKnock! It's Rafael." He laughed alone because I no longer felt like laughing.

Madalena opened the door and smiled with that idiotic expression she put on when she looked at older men.

"*¡Buenas*! *¿La abuela*?"

"She's right here."

"Let's go, then. Come with me." He took my hand, which was another thing I didn't like.

"Good day, Doctor. Forgive me for not getting up."

"Don't worry."

"Madalena, offer the doctor a drink."

"That would—"

"A glass of water, good and cold," Granma Nhé interrupted.

"That would be very nice."

"But, as there's no electricity, we only have water without ice. Anyway, ice water is bad for the throat."

"I understand." With a gentle laugh, Comrade Rafael began to take instruments out of his bag. "We are going to measure your *tensión*."

"As you wish. Do you want the child to leave?"

"No, no. He is a brave *compañero*, no?"

"*Sí.*"

"All right. A little *silencio, por favor.*"

"Unplug the radio, Madalena."

"I can't, Granma."

"Turn off the radio, you hear me?"

Rafael KnockKnock strained to hear the heartbeat as everybody kept talking.

"But, Granma, the 'off' button broke."

"Then take out the batteries, you dimwit. Is your head just for hanging braids?"

The radio went off, but the parrots in the yard started to shout. "Citizens of Sucupira," one of them screeched in the voice of old Odorico. "The bloodythirsty bandit Roque Santeiro, son of a snoring, snorting mare," the other shouted in the voice of Sinhozinho Malta. Comrade Rafael almost had to close his eyes to try to hear. The rooster crowed, too, and Senhor Tuarles began to press down on the accelerator of the broken-down car in his yard. The car didn't work any more, but Senhor Tuarles liked to rev it up.

"How's it look, Doctor?"

"Everything *está bien* with *la tensión,* don't worry, *Abuela.* I've come to talk to you about something else—something more serious."

"What's that?"

"He said he came to talk about something else, Granma."

"*Gracias, muchacho.* Tell your *abuela* that I spoke with Victoria, her daughter..."

"Aunty Tó fought her?"

"No, I spoke to your aunt, who asked me—" Here Comrade Rafael KnockKnock did what the Cubans, and also the Soviets, always did: he started to speak more slowly but also more loudly to see whether I understood.

"Son, tell the doctor that in our house we don't like people to speak so loudly."

"I am sorry, Señora Agnette. I spoke with your daughter Victoria, who asked me to come and explain to you the seriousness of your *condición.*"

"My what?"

"Aunty Tó told him to come here to give you news, Granma, because I guess Aunty Tó doesn't have the courage to come here and tell you the news herself."

"Don't start inventing things," Granma Nhé said.

"I didn't invent anything, Granma. Let him tell you what's going on."

"*Bueno*...It turns out *la situación* is more *complicada* than I had thought."

"He's saying the situation's real complicated, Granma."

"You have a wound that is... How do you say, gangrenaded."

"Granma, he says your wound is like a grenade."

"No, no, *muchacho*, 'gangrenaded' is a technical term."

"But that grenade is just a technical term. He means it won't dexplode."

"No, look, *muchacho*, seriously, you have to tell her: the wound is very bad and it is very dangerous."

"The wound has a lot of danger and is really bad."

"Oh my God." Granma Nhé looked worried, the poor thing.

"It's too late, we can do *nada* and it is very dangerous for it to stay like this. She will have to go to the hospital *mañana* and have an operation."

"Operation?" Granma asked.

"Yes, Granma. He says the wound's dangerous and they have to operate tomorrow."

"I'm not leaving this house until I speak to my daughter."

"*Sí*. I *comprendo* but I have already spoken to your daughter. She is in the military hospital preparing everything."

"He said he's already spoken with Aunty Tó, that she's in the military hospital to prepare things, Granma."

"Very good." Granma Nhé took a deep breath. "Drink your glass of water slowly."

"*¿Cómo?*"

"Drink your water slowly. Slowly. I've already had one person making my life miserable over a glass of water."

Comrade Rafael KnockKnock looked at me in search of an explanation that I was unable to provide.

"Drink the water, Comrade. It's from the filter and it contains lye. You can drink it without worry."

"I understand."

"Now you can go, Doctor." Granma spoke slowly. "I need to be alone."

"*Bueno, Abuela*, as you wish. We will see each other *mañana*. Take care."

"Thank you."

Madalena picked up the glass of water and I went to accompany Comrade Rafael to his car.

"Look, tell your Aunt Victoria that she must prepare her better. Psychologically, I mean."

"What do you mean? What do I say?"

"She must speak with her. You see, *mañana* we have to remove her toe. If we don't do it, there's a danger that she'll lose her foot and her whole leg. You have to be strong, *muchacho. Adiós.*"

"*Adiós.*"

Outside, Charlita and 3.14 were looking at me with fearful expressions.

"Did you understand what he said?"

"I guess so."

"And you aren't going to tell your granma?"

"I guess she already understood. We'll talk later."

When I entered the house Granma Nhé was on the telephone with tears in her eyes, talking to Aunty Tó, who was also a doctor, and who must have been explaining everything to her. I heard the sound of the windows being closed and I thought that it was about time for Granma Catarina to appear.

Granma hung up the phone, wiped her tears and pulled me close to her.

"I don't like to see you cry, Granma."

"I'm over it now, son. Your granma's not going to cry anymore. Aunty Tó will come here at lunchtime. She says she's bringing a special little feast and that after she'll explain everything."

Granma Catarina appeared in the living room with her shawl over her head.

"Catarina! You gave me a fright."

"Everything's going to go fine, Sis, don't worry. What did Tó say to you?"

"I didn't understand her explanation at all, but they say they're going to have to cut off my toe. They say it's all infected."

"Aren't you afraid, Granma?"

She made a face like someone who was afraid but wanted to hide it.

"It's not necessary to be afraid." Granma Catarina touched me, the way she used to a long time ago. "They're just going to cut off a toe, she'll still have lots left. Life's like that, son."

It feels wrong to talk like this, but in Luanda having a granma who's in danger of losing a toe conjures up meals that you usually just dream about and wouldn't find anywhere.

Aunty Tó arrived with her husband and over the course of the afternoon other people began appearing, relatives or close friends, nephews or cousins-who-were-like-brothers. Each of them brought something to eat or drink. The table started to fill up with such appetizing treats that they had to forbid the children from coming close prior to the official opening of the meal.

We didn't really have lunch that day. When Aunty Tó arrived she explained to Granma Nhé that Comrade Rafael KnockKnock was an "excellent" doctor—that was what she said—an ace in operations related to that word that sounded like grenade, and turned out to be "gangrened," and that she herself had been at the meetings at the military hospital and the longer we waited the worse it would be. Comrade Rafael's suggestion of operating the next day had been accepted by everyone; all that remained was for Granma Nhé to say yes.

"I'll do whatever you think is best, daughter." Granma Catarina sat halfway up the stairs, looking at me while she listened to the conversation, and laid her finger on her lips as a signal to me to not tell anyone that she was there. "They can cut off as many of my toes as they like. There's just one thing I'm going to promise you: you will never see me with a cane. Not even if I have to spend the rest of my days locked up in my room."

"Oh, Mother, don't exaggerate. It's just a toe, and your other toes are so crooked you won't even notice that they've cut one off."

"I repeat: they can cut off as many toes as they wish, as long as I can squeeze my foot into my shoe so that nobody sees. But no cane. Nor crutches. That would be all I need: to have my late husband see me at this age, walking with crutches."

"May I schedule the operation, Mother?"

Granma Nhé looked at me, but it wasn't me she wanted to talk to. I made a sign to Granma Catarina, who came down two steps. Granma Catarina smiled.

"Mother?"

"You can schedule it. But today we're going to have a party."

"A party, Mother?"

"Yes, ask your brothers and sisters to bring food and wine. Isn't the operation tomorrow?"

"Yes, it is."

"Then today we're going to have a farewell party for my toe."

Granma Catarina laughed and began to climb the stairs slowly, without making a sound.

"Come here, son," Granma Nhé called me. "Go tell your Granma's friends that late this afternoon we're going to have special snacks here. But don't tell them anything else."

"Sure, Granma. Can the kids from the street come, too?"

"Yes they can."

Once she had made her sudden decision to throw a real farewell party for her toe, Granma Nhé was in a good mood. She didn't even bawl out Madalena Kamussekele for not yet having tidied up the kitchen at this late hour; she simply ordered her to go to the Blue District to look for some delicious patties that had shrimp inside them instead of just cream. Then she put in an order with Granma Maria, Charlita's granma, for two orders of freshly cooked *kitaba*, one with hot peppers and the other without; she requested of the Old Fisherman that he bring fresh *quitetas* that someone was going to prepare. When Dona Libânia came to see if she was better, she found Granma Nhé walking with difficulty but saying that she could no longer sit down, to the point of laughing at this suggestion. In the street, we bought sweet pastries that had just come out of the oven at Samba's store and then Dona Libânia said she was going to make her famous banana cake, which was enormous and filled the stomach even of a person who ate only half a slice.

The rest was brought by relatives. "The spread looked pretty," as Granma Nhé liked to say. There were wines of all colours. I even heard the names: white wine—I was already familiar with that one—"well-aged red wine"—I didn't even know that wine had to age—and even something called "rosé" that Comrade Rafael KnockKnock really liked a lot, and that made him start to talk like anything at the end of the party.

Almost all of Bishop's Beach came, and everybody laughed when they heard that it was an impromptu party whose purpose was to bid farewell to a toe that was going to be removed the next day. It was funny, and when somebody didn't believe her, Granma Nhé called on Comrade Rafael who was already completely loaded and before he began to speak, even without a door, would say, "KnockKnock!" and then confirm the matter, saying that it was because of its being "gangrenated," and somebody still asked, "A grenade?" He would laugh and wink at me: "No, no. It's gangrene, we have to remove her toe as quickly as possible." Even Father João Domingo showed up, and Granma Nhé asked him if it was necessary to bless the toe in order for the operation to go well.

"No, Dona Agnette. If it were the birth of a toe, we would do a small baptism. Now, under these conditions, I think this party will be sufficient. The main thing is that you have a positive outlook."

"That I do." Granma Nhé shared a toast with the priest.

The party went on because that's the way it was: until all the drinks and all the food had been finished nobody was going to leave. The Old Fisherman's *quitetas* were a wonder with lemon sauce, and people even mixed white wine with hot peppers. When the children's *kitaba* ran out we attacked the elders' spicy *kitaba*. The trick was to drink a mouthful of milk right after and then it didn't sting any more. Everybody said that Dona Libânia's cake was a marvel; it was enormous and she had put something powerful in the cake because it was unusual for anyone to manage to eat more than a slice. Everybody was in high spirits with the Cuban music they were playing on National Radio. Two or three couples were already dancing; outside, in the yard, we played hide-and-seek and tag. The parrots started to talk nonsense because things were getting too wild for them. "*Cabrón,*" one was saying. "*Hijo de puta,*" said the other. They went on like that the whole night. It must have been from some film because those parrots only knew words from soap operas or films. "My nayme eez no-bodee," was from a Trinità film. "And here's the news," was the voice of the eight o'clock anchor, "Rosebud" was from a show, "Ametista... Ametista..." was the voice of Sinhozinho Malta in the episode where Zé das Medalhas kills Sinhozinho's cow, and at times they even sang, "*Del barco del Chanquete, no nos moverán,*" which was a song from *Blue Summer*, and in the midst of all this confusion, I think the radio's batteries died, and when somebody went to change them, there was a knock on the door.

Sea Foam, who was in the yard with us, looked terrified and took off running towards his house. There was another knock. I looked up at the second floor. Granma Catarina, who hadn't come down since the beginning of the party, was at the window. She just smiled.

"It must be the Soviet."

So it was. He was frightened by the crowd in the living room, with all of them staring at him. He came in slowly and spent a long time cleaning his dust-laden boots.

"Gudafter-noon."

As everyone was already a bit sloshed, they answered with the same accent: "Gudafter-noon."

The music started again. He entered and asked for Granma Nhé, who was getting some more dishes ready in the kitchen. When Granma Nhé came into the living room, his smile disappeared from his mouth in an instant. Granma Nhé regarded Comrade Gudafterov with a strange look.

"Take it easy, Mother," Aunty Tó urged.

"Gudafter-noon, Dona Nhéte. You don't haf light again? Bilhardov put cable."

Granma made her way slowly to his side.

"Good evening, Comrade Bilhardov. Are you coming from a funeral?"

"Fooneral? I no understand."

"You have flowers in your hand. You must be coming from a funeral. What a shame you forgot to leave the flowers there."

"Bilhardov no understand."

It was Aunty Tó who saved Comrade Gudafterov. She smiled at him. "Don't worry, my mother's had a couple of drinks." She took the flowers from his hand, thanked him and carried them to the kitchen.

Granma Nhé, as everybody knows, doesn't like to be given flowers. She says it reminds her of funerals and cemeteries.

Comrade Gudafterov, without even noticing, found himself in a confusing situation, but then his confusion deepened because someone had brought vodka and he rapidly downed seven shots in a row.

"Tomorrow Bilhardov fix cable again. Dona Nhéte's house haf light from Mausoleum. *Viva*!"

In the kitchen, Aunty Tó was about to drop the flowers into the garbage.

"Don't do that, daughter."

"But, Mother, you don't like being given flowers."

"No, I don't like it. But this time I'm going to make use of them."

"Make use of them to do what, Mother?"

"Tomorrow I want to go to the cemetery."

"Tomorrow's the day of your operation, Mother."

"But before, I want to go to the cemetery. Leave the flowers there in the corner."

Aunty Tó left the kitchen and went to say goodbye to some people who were leaving. Madalena came in.

"Madalena, get a vase for those flowers."

"Should I put them in the living room, Granma?"

"Don't even think of it. Put them outside in the yard."

Granma Nhé remained standing, her eyes gleaming with a slow light. She looked outside, but in a direction where it was impossible to see the light or the stars. I didn't understand where she was looking.

"Granma."

"Yes, son."

"Can I go to the cemetery with you tomorrow?"

"You want to?"

"Yes."

"Yes, you can."

"Can Granma Catarina come with us, Granma?"

Granma Nhé laughed to herself, gave me an affectionate pat and told me to go play a little longer. Aunty Tó came back into the kitchen with a laugh.

"What is it, daughter?" Granma Nhé wiped at her bright eyes.

"I just came to give you a kiss, Mother. Everything's going to be fine. I think you're wonderful."

"That's good, daughter."

"Now you won't be my little mother any more."

"What do you mean?"

"You'll be my little nineteener, Mother. You're only going to have nineteen fingers and toes."

They both burst out laughing with a happiness that startled me. As Sea Foam said, "Words have magical charms and invisible strengths." It's true: that little gibe about being a "nineteener" not only made Granma Nhé laugh again but it changed her name for the rest of her life.

It was that night, on Bishop's Beach, that Granma Agnette became Granma Nineteen.

I had that dream many times, but not with so many kids running along Bishop's Beach without the strings of their kites getting tangled up—like crazy knots in the Comrade Old Fisherman's net—nor had I seen so much wind causing such a strong swell in such a calm sea, it was just that when I dreamed I didn't know it was a dream: my breathing became rushed because I was upset at seeing the square and the gas station with so many children and I wanted to know who they were. The children from Bishop's Beach were there and also those from the Blue District, others from school and even a few adults: Aunt Adelaide laughing, the Comrade Gas Jockey running with a red and yellow kite, even Uncle Rui, who was a writer, went past on a bicycle that had moustaches drawn on it, and he did two things at once, riding the bike and keeping the kite under control—what a beautiful bicycle!—and Senhor Tuarles had a mug of beer in one hand and with the other he made the kites feint like soccer players, even Comrade Gudafterov was laughing and running, "Dona Nhéte, ka-yet bring news from far-away," but what had never before happened to me in that dream of carnivals and also laughter was to see so many animated colours in a dance of soaring winds and the sky full of a thousand greens, yellows, oranges and reds with the blue behind, the sky imitating some birds that might be the living body of what's called a rainbow.

"Are you dreaming, son?"

"Ay, Granma, don't wake me up like that, I was dreaming about an awesome rainbow."

"Oh, my dear,"—she wiped my face—"you were breathing so fast and covered in sweat. I was afraid you were having an asthma attack."

"It was a many-coloured asthma, Granma...Our sky here on Bishop's Beach had colours that I don't even know how to describe to you."

"The same dream, then."

"But with 'multiplication factors,' as they say at my school."

"It's time to wake up in any event. Are you coming with me to the cemetery?"

"Yes. Are you going to talk with Granpa Mbinha?"

"It's not the place to talk, son. It's just to be there for a while. Sometimes a person goes to the cemetery to talk to herself."

"Sea Foam talks to himself without going to the cemetery."

We lingered over breakfast: a really good black tea that Madalena mixed with verbena leaf; the first time she had done that everybody refused to drink it, and now it was a custom and was even offered to visitors.

"There wasn't any bread today, Granma," Madalena explained.

"That's all right. Heat up a bit of yesterday's bread in the oven, it tastes wonderful. Just for five minutes so we don't waste gas."

"Yes, Granma."

It was very early. The windows could still be opened without the risk of our having a breakfast of bread and butter with a light covering of dust.

The chickens were demanding the corn that hadn't appeared for three days. They were just eating stale bread and potato peelings left over from someone's house.

At that hour of the morning, Granma Catarina didn't appear. The parrots didn't talk nonsense before eleven o'clock. I put this in a school composition and the Comrade Teacher told me not to lie because lies were vile. She even ordered me to write another composition. Since it was on a topic of my choice, I wrote about Granma Nhé's friend Carmen Fernández, with her pregnancy of a bag of ants and another of a bird-baby, and the teacher threatened to beat me with her ruler and asked whether I knew how to write normal compositions like other children, like perhaps about a trip or a relative.

I swear that I made an effort, and I thought it would be a good idea to write about a journey I'd made to Benguela, where my Uncle Victor said that he had an enormous swimming pool full of Coca-Cola, and about how I had felt really sorry because we children had been told that Granma Catarina couldn't come with us. I was scolded again just the same and my mother was even summoned to the parent-teacher meeting because the Comrade Teacher knew the family and said that it might be possible that a crazy uncle had filled a swimming pool with Coca Cola, but what was impossible was my having written that Granma Catarina could have accompanied us because the Comrade Teacher knew that Granma Catarina hadn't lived in that house for many years.

So as not to appear undisciplined, I remained silent when the Comrade Teacher ordered me to tear up the three compositions, but I felt like laughing because of course Uncle Victor didn't have enough Coca Cola to fill a swimming pool, but we all knew that Granma Catarina was in Granma Nhé's house; she even opened and closed windows. It was just that she didn't like to appear very early in the day or when there were strangers in the house, but that didn't mean that she wouldn't have wanted to go with us to Benguela.

"What are you thinking about, son? Finish your bread."

"About a composition I wrote... Granma Catarina was in it. I still think she didn't go to Benguela just because nobody invited her."

"Finish your bread, son. Today I have to go to the hospital to have a toe removed."

"And after that we're really going to call you Granma Nineteen?"

"I suppose so."

We were just about to leave. Granma Nhé's bag was ready, with her nice silk nightgown and her Chinese slippers.

Granma looked slowly around at the whole room—the windows, the carpet, the beat-up brown sofa, the really old wood-framed television, the photos on the walls—and stopped to look at the display cabinet containing the pretty Chinese tea service.

"The first granddaughter who makes a proper marriage gets that tea service. We'll see who it is."

"These days nobody marries as a virgin." Granma Catarina appeared out of nowhere.

"Catarina, I'm going to the hospital. But first I'm going to the cemetery."

"Take advantage of the opportunity to tell your grandson the truth."

"I'll only be back tomorrow morning, if the doctor lets me."

"The truth, Agnette. You have to tell the children the truth."

"Goodbye, Sis. Till tomorrow."

"Goodbye."

"See you, Granma Catarina."

"See you, son. Look after your Granma."

Granma Nhé went out carrying her bag. Senhor Osório, who was going to give us a lift, had already honked twice. Granma Catarina stayed near the door to watch me while I went down the steps of the veranda.

"Even if you don't see me, I'm nearby. Life is also made up of things that we don't know how to explain but which are always there."

"I didn't understand anything, but I'm going to give you a kiss."

Granma Catarina didn't leave the doorway. It was as if there were a fox trap there that she couldn't tread on. She looked in the direction of the enormous trees of Dona Libânia's house, and she smiled.

"You see the mills?"

"Those are trees, Granma Catarina. Big, beautiful trees."

"But they look like mills of time."

"I'm sorry, Granma. It's just I don't know what mills are and I'm really late."

"They're big spades that help to push time forward."

"What pushes time forward, at least as I've seen it being pushed, are the hands of the clock," I shouted as I ran for the car.

"It's the same, my dear."

We went in Senhor Osório's car. He was already pretty much a friend of the family and drove a white Opel that ran on diesel fuel. Before turning the key in the ignition, it was necessary to wait for a pretty blue light that came on; only after that was the car warmed up. I met Senhor Osório when I was little and he used to visit Uncle Chico at his house with the wonderfully chilled beer that came out of the faucet installed in the wall.

"Are you all right?"

"Good, thanks, Senhor Osório."

"Ready to go for a spin?"

He always drew a deep breath—I'd never seen a person who made so much noise with his breathing—once the blue light came on. He started the car. That Opel was pretty: all white, and always freshly polished and washed. Senhor Osório actually worked for Opel and I guess he must have washed his car several times a day; at least I never saw it dirty. Seated, he succeeded in straightening his slacks, that's to say, everybody knew that Senhor Osório was notorious as "slacks-up-to-his-armpits" because he pulled his slacks up until they almost touched his armpit, in spite of his handsome belly and wide suspenders.

"We're going to High Cross Cemetery, please, Senhor Osório."

"All right, Dona Agnette."

I opened the window to sniff the odours from the sea because we were certain to follow the shore of Bishop's Beach, that's to say, close to the sea, and after the Fortress we were going to turn onto the Marginal, and since Senhor Osório drove really slowly, I had time to say hi to Charlita and 3.14, who shouted, "Good luck." The Comrade Gas Jockey waved a languid goodbye, Sea Foam was at his house's front gate, fanning his leg with his whip and a chain in the other hand; the church was closed, but a few cleaning ladies were sweeping the dusty patio, though I don't know why they bothered to sweep it since the same dust was going to return to the same places. On the lefthand side was the calm, peaceful sea with the sun's patterned light shining on it and some fishermen going out to fish. Then came the Marginal—the wide street of the Marginal—still with only a few cars, and the beautiful building of the National Bank of Angola, and when we got close to the Nazaré Church, we curved to take the Eixo Viário, this time in the direction of the cemetery.

"Are you coming in with us, Senhor Osório?"

"No, Dona Agnette. I'm not in the habit of entering cemeteries."

"What will you do the day your mother passes away?"

"My dear mother is already deceased, Dona Agnette."

"You didn't go to the burial?"

"I was here in Angola. She died in Portugal."

When we arrived there were lots of ladies outside the cemetery selling flowers of all colours, those really big ones that they put on the coffin once it's closed and other, smaller ones to be carried in the hand or offered to those who cry the most. As it was a weekday, there wasn't much crying or wailing going on.

"Instead of planting flowers in gardens, they bring them to cemeteries where nobody cares any more."

"Don't you like flowers, Granma?"

"I like them, son, but I like to see them in gardens and along the streets to give life some colour. Death hasn't got any colour, son."

"Granma Catarina says that, too."

"Let's go in. Can you manage to carry that big bottle?"

"I can carry it, Granma."

The big bottle of water was to clean off Granpa Mbinha's headstone, which was filthy because Granma Nhé only came to visit it once a year, on Granpa's birthday.

"Let's go look for the headstone. I never know exactly where it is."

I liked this part because, to tell the truth, I think this was just Granma Nhé playing around. She knew very well where the headstone was; even I could almost get there with my eyes closed. But that was how this worked: we went wandering around and stumbling over other headstones and she told me little tales. I never completely understood whether this was a way to make me aware of certain things, or whether it was just to tame her own sad yearning for people she hadn't seen in a long time. "This headstone belongs to the late Don Tito, Carmen Fernández's father, who died of heartbreak when he learned about her giving birth to the bag of ants." She poured out a few drops of water, arranged the dry but pretty flowers that someone had left there a long time ago. "Here lies the late Barradas, father of that Barradas who was famous all the way to the Workers' District for being excessively endowed." I didn't really understand. "Endowed, Granma?" She smiled, wiping the tears from her eyes. "One day Granma will tell you the tale of how Barradas got ready to play soccer and then the tale of the blind woman who started shouting." She blew on other headstones, looked at the little photographs behind broken glass, brushed away leaves. "Here's Senhor Santos, Granma Chica's husband. Yes, they sure had a nice wine cellar. Clean that photograph well." The gravediggers started to approach us to ask if we needed help. Granma didn't want any help, she was even willing to give them money, but Granma Nhé didn't like to have a lot of people around her in the cemetery.

We found Granpa Mbinha's headstone. It was actually clean; it had rained a little while ago. We swept around the sides, Granma blew away the dust and cleaned the black-and-white photograph that Granpa must have had taken without knowing that he was going to die because he had a really important air, with his head tilted, looking upwards. Granpa Mbhina was handsome and something about him reminded me of the Indians in movies.

"My Cachimbinha is handsome, don't you think?"

"Really handsome, Granma."

"The women who were after him! Leave it, son... I had to be very careful. This Granpa of yours was a scoundrel."

"Granma, why did they call him Cachimbinha?"

"Because of that other Cachimbinha, the soccer player."

"Granpa liked soccer?"

"He loved it, and he played it very well."

"My Granpa Aníbal told me that when he was young they played soccer with a ball made from a pig's bladder."

"A pig's bladder be damned! That must have been back where he came from."

"I don't know, Granma. Maybe it was in the really, really olden days."

Granma Nhé fell silent. She put her hands together at the front of her waist and began to pretend that she was praying. Her lips were moving and I made an effort to understand the text, but it wasn't possible, there was just a murmuring—shh, shh, shh. I only heard a few words from the Lord's Prayer, and the "Amen," at the end. And then Granma Nhé was at peace.

Elders do that, it's normal. I don't like to be at peace very much, but sometimes it happens. It was good there, like a film that couldn't be shown any more: the gravediggers kept their distance but they stopped digging and remained silent, the trees swayed more gently, and there was a noise in the sky made by birds that came in to land in those peaceful trees, very old trees, because cemeteries, as everyone knows, are very old places, and, "Lots of people have already died in this world," as Granma Catarina said. The sky was turning all blue and it was almost cloudless, even the few clouds that were visible were at a standstill; only Granma Nhé's hair was moving a touch, as if it were flying.

The letters on Granpa Mbinha's headstone were very small and had been worn down by time and the sun. It was almost impossible to read them. There was another name there, not the main name, but a name from the family. I tried to ask Granma Nhé who it was, but she had a little tear falling from her eye, and I stayed silent.

"Let's go, son. I can't put up any more with the pain in my foot."

"You want me to call Senhor Osório with his slacks up to his armpits?"

Granma laughed.

"No, that's not necessary. You help me yourself."

"Granma, do you come here to talk to Granpa Mbinha?"

"I suppose I do."

"Can the dead hear what we say?"

"Some of them can."

The gravediggers said goodbye and thanked Granma for the money she had given them. The birds made their starting-to-fly noise and the trees stirred a little. The walls inside the cemetery were all white; it was true that it was a pleasant spot for a person to spend half an hour not doing anything.

"Granma, can more than one person be buried beneath the same headstone?"

"Yes." She stopped and stood looking at me with her eyes very open and moist.

"I saw two names there, Granma."

"I know, son."

"Is there another person buried there, Granma?"

"There is."

In that moment a great silence struck my heart. I looked into Granma Nhé's pretty eyes; her face was telling me that I could ask her a thousand more questions and she would answer them for me, but my heart silenced me. It took the words out of my mouth and I was left without any more questions to ask. Just like that.

"Are you coming to drop me at the hospital?"

"Yes I am, Granma."

She had kept a tiny flower in her handbag. She took it out gradually and set it in my hand.

"Did you forget it? Do you want me to go put it over there?"

"I want you to keep it for yourself."

"All right." I put it in my shirt pocket so as not to crush it. "Granma?"

"Tell me, my dear."

"I like you a lot." Granma didn't reply and kept walking, but she held my hand with a soft grip. "I like our conversations a lot, even when sometimes we don't manage to say anything."

"You're a darling. And when you grow up,"—she lowered her head to speak with me, looking me in the eyes with a peaceful gaze—"when you grow up, you have to remember all of these tales. Inside you. You promise?"

"Yes, Granma." I didn't even know what she meant, but with the open wound in her foot hurting her, and with her on the point of being hospitalized for an operation to have something cut off, I figured it was a good idea just to promise everything. "And you, Granma, do you promise to give me an ice cream when you come out of the hospital?"

"I promise."

Senhor Osório looked like a chauffeur in a black-and-white movie: he went around the back and opened the door for Granma Nhé to get in.

"Can we go on, Dona Agnette?"

"We can, thank you very much, Senhor Osório. We're going to the military hospital."

Everyone was silent during the drive. Senhor Osório was whistling, it must have been because his indicators didn't work; he whistled before he made a turn. All he had to do was go and see a mechanic. Everybody knows that when the indicators don't work it's something to do with a fuse, and you've just got to change it, a fuse that's not needed for another light can be installed there; but I didn't say a word, so that Senhor Osório wouldn't think I was setting myself up as an expert.

At the entrance to the military hospital there was a barrier with military comrades who kept tabs on everybody who came in. They asked us what we were doing there.

"The vehicle can't enter, Comrade."

"What do you mean it can't? I'm going to take this lady to have an operation, she can't walk."

"An operation on what?"

"On her leg."

"On a toe," Granma Nhé corrected.

"On a leg or a toe?"

"On the toe, Comrade. Let us in, we're already late."

"Is the operation being performed by a doctor, and who is he?"

"Doctor Rafael KnockKnock," I snapped.

"KnockKnock? I've never heard of him."

"Please, Comrade, " Granma said, "don't make us waste time. It's an emergency case. Doctor Rafael is going to cut off my toe."

"A toe?"

"That's right."

"And are you gonna walk okay after that, ma'am?"

"Yes, I will. Inside my shoe it won't even be noticeable."

"Do you know where the operating block is?"

"Yes, I know." Senhor Osório started to whistle and put on the indicator even though the indicator didn't work.

"Go ahead, please. Have a good operation, ma'am. They cut my brother's whole leg off, he needs crutches to walk. Even so, he still dances at parties."

Inside, Comrade Rafael KnockKnock was laughing as he waited for Granma Nhé.

"KnockKnock," he joked as he rapped on the door of the car. "*¿Cómo está, abuela*? Everything *bien*?"

"Yes. This is Senhor Osório."

"*Encantado*. Are you staying for *la operación*?"

"No, no, I have to go take care of some business. Good luck, Dona Agnette. Your daughter should be in there. I'll wait outside to take the little boy home."

"Okay. Yes, your daughter's inside and we have a little *sorpresa*."

"More surprises?"

"Only *una*. You are going to like it."

Senhor Osório got out of the car even though Granma's door was already open. He pulled his slacks up even higher, until his suspenders were completely limp, wiped his sweat with a white handkerchief and stood watching us while we entered the hospital.

"I've learned that I can't give *flores* to the *señorita*,"—Comrade Rafael was smiling—"but there is something I want to give her."

This must have been the waiting room for the operations. Aunty Tó was there, already dressed in the really ugly green gown worn in operating rooms. A clapped-out old apparatus with pretenses to being a turntable and two columns stood on a shelf.

"If you will do me *el honor*..." Comrade Rafael KnockKnock made a gesture in the air with his hand. I figured it was for Granma to dance with him.

Granma Nhé accepted with a smile.

"I don't know if I'm up to this, doctor."

"*Sí*, you are. Don't worry. A last *baile* before the procedure."

Music from the movies was playing. I already knew that sound, pretty and calm. Some nurses came to listen and stood still, watching while Granma danced with the doctor. Aunty Tó's eyes were moist; I don't know if she was afraid, or she simply felt like crying. With difficulty but in good spirits, Granma started to dance to that music from the past—then I knew what it was: a tango.

"That's so that when you are better, *bailamos* again. You are going to see what beautiful *trabajo* we are going to do here. I just need you to be *tranquila, Abuela.*"

"Thank you, doctor. I never thought I would dance a tango in the waiting room at the military hospital."

"Life is full of *sorpresas, señora* Agnette."

They were dancing as if time had stopped on all of the hospital's clocks.

Other patients, in bed, on crutches, in filthy gowns, with tired eyes and dishevelled hair, with plasters on their arms, wearing grimy glasses, and other doctors in white and green gowns, even two security guards, came to take a good look at the dance that seemed to go on forever. Aunty Tó, her arms crossed, let her body bob from side to side; her eyes travelled far away. I can understand this: even I, being there, hearing that music, remembered a film I'd seen, the couple who danced in the film, a little more rapidly, it's true, but it was also necessary to see that Granma had a wound in her toe and, with her steps, couldn't twirl around any more than she was doing already.

"Now it's time." Comrade Rafael spoke gently as the music ended. "We are going to do our *trabajo*. One toe, *nada más*, I promise you. You will have nineteen digits left."

Granma blew me a kiss from her hand as she smiled. I figure that the dancing had done her good, her face looked calmer and she even walked better.

As Sea Foam used to say, it was the miracle of music.

"My feet know the truth that my heart feels when my ears smile. Music is the miracle the Communists already authorized, ha-ha-ha! Let's *bailar, compañeros*!"

Senhor Osório dropped me off on Bishop's Beach. I couldn't get that tango music out of my head. The Comrade Gas Jockey waved me goodbye and I stood at the gate of Granma Nhé's house.

"How's it goin', everything okay?" 3.14 asked.

"Everything's cool."

"And your Granma?"

"She's in the operating room."

"Did you really go to the hospital?"

"I went. It's a hospital where they play tango music before they operate on people."

"Quit tellin' fibs."

"I swear. You can ask my Granma later."

"Look, what are we gonna do now?"

"What do you mean? It's almost lunchtime."

"But didn't we agree that we were going to take care of the marks on the sidewalks? Charlita's already got some paint thinner."

"You figure paint thinner'll take it out?"

"Yeah, it takes it out. We already tried with one and it took it out."

"Except they must know by heart the houses they want to dexplode."

"Even so. This is just the beginning of our plan to slow them down. Afterwards, we have to find a way to do the rest."

"The rest?"

"Just go have your lunch and we'll meet afterwards. It's a really risky plan, we can't tell very many people about it."

"But what kind of plan is it?"

"I figure we're going to have to do things that the elders are never going to be able to find out about. Are you going to keep this secret?"

"Yes."

"Me, too. Charlita promised, too. Just go eat. We'll talk later."

At the table, Madalena was serving tasty leftovers from the party to some cousins who had slept over. I told them all about the outing to the cemetery and nobody believed me, that beneath Granpa Mbinha's headstone another person was buried there as if his neighbour, but that they were in the same plot, that I just couldn't tell them the name because I hadn't managed to read it. I also told them about Comrade Rafael KnockKnock and his waiting room tango playing and they called me a liar because neither the guards nor the Comrade Director would let music be played near the operating room. On top of that, Senhor Osório hadn't stayed with us for lunch to confirm the situation.

"It's obvious you're making things up," Madalena said. "Just shut up and eat so flies don't get into your mouth."

"You shut up. You never saw the military hospital or heard the tango."

"You watch out, or I'll tell about the wire cutters."

"You watch out, or I'll tell about the coarse salt."

Madalena turned quiet and went into the kitchen. We ate quickly. I asked about Granma Catarina, but everyone remained silent. Afterwards I saw Madalena in the kitchen putting the rest of the leftovers into plastic bags.

"What are you doing that for, Madalena?"

"None of your business."

I didn't know why, if it was a holiday or what, or if there was a workers' assembly, but the Mausoleum construction site was practically empty. Charlita and 3.14 had offered the guard who was on duty leftover vodka from the toe's farewell party, which was even mixed with wine. The guard was soon snoring over on the beach, curled up against Rainboat.

The main gate was open, but 3.14 figured that it was better for us to go in on the other side, where there was already a hole in the metal grating.

We ran with our hearts beating really fast, and I didn't even really know what the plan was.

"The plan is that we find all of the dynamite."

"And then?"

"Then we hide it and they can't blow up Bishop's Beach."

We entered the storage shed that smelled of mould and heard the noise of hens clucking. We took the lid off one box, then a second one, and the incredibly skinny hens stood watching us as though we were obliged to give them corn.

"It must not be here."

"Wait, there's a ton of boxes, it could be in the others."

"Hey, 3.14, you guys are draggin' those boxes all over the place. Are you sure they won't dexplode on their own?"

"Didn't you ever see a Trinità movie? Dynamite only dexplodes when you light the fuzz."

"The fuse, you retard."

We opened more boxes and they contained tiny little cages that hardly left the creatures inside space to budge. We all looked at one another: there were pretty birds of colours a person doesn't often even have in his crayon set, those purple colours mixed with dark blue or toasted yellow, lots of tiny little birds with colourful beaks and a heap –and I mean a heap—of parrots that said words in really difficult Soviet.

"Let's split. It can't be here."

"And the birds?" Charlita stood looking at them.

"I'm not the birds' godfather."

"But aren't they going to die here?"

"Let's just go." 3.14 pulled Charlita's arm. "Birds can last for days without eating."

"And without seeing any light?"

"They can last. Don't you know that bats don't even like to see the sun?"

"Bats are birds?"

"Come on! Let's just go. You guys are screwing up the operation."

We took off without closing the door. Charlita asked us to leave it like that, "so that at least they can get a breath of air." We had to hide when we heard a noise nearby, but it was just a blue lobster peeing, and after he was done he left and went over to a huge tent where that assembly must be taking place.

We discovered that there was another entrance to the storage shed. On one side there were just the tools and clothing for the site, the workers' monkey suits, demijohns of wine and bottles of vodka, helmets and a few Soviet guards' uniforms. 3.14 found a pair of garden shears and started to cut up the sleeves of the tunics.

"What are you doing that for?" Charlita was really nervous.

"So they can get used to the fact that this is a hot country and not wander around all bundled up like they're in the snow. Hahaha!"

We heard the sound of military boots and had just enough time to hide behind the tractor.

"We're going to have to beat a retreat."

"What are we going to beat it with?" Charlita wanted to know.

"You see? Your problem is that you don't watch movies, and then you want to go on missions with boys."

"Keep your voice down or they're going to catch us."

"You don't know military codes, or what a 'strategic retreat' is."

"Isn't that just runnin' away?"

"Yeah, but you have to say retreat. Beating a retreat."

The soldiers were drunk and sat down right in the doorway of the storage shed. We were terrified when one of them leaned against the door and fell over backwards with the door wide open. The other laughed, and gave us time to see some suspicious boxes.

"The boxes with the dynamite!"

"How do you know?"

"It's totally obvious that you don't watch movies. They've got the symbol on the side."

"What symbol?"

"The symbol for dynamite."

"Draw it in the sand so I can see it."

"It doesn't work in the sand. We're gonna have to split as soon as they fall asleep."

We went out of the site through the hole in the metal grating. We took a turn on the beach so that nobody would be suspicious.

"Everything all right, kids?" It was the Old Fisherman.

"Everything all right, Elder. We just went to visit the blue lobsters."

"That's good. But don't tell Granma."

"Okay."

We ran to the old chicken coop at Charlita's house, where they had hidden the paint thinner. If there weren't many people in the street there would still be time to complete the mission of blotting out the marks on the sidewalks.

As we were about to leave with the materials, Senhor Tuarles caught us.

"Good afternoon, kids. Are you playing here in Granma Maria's chicken coop?"

"No, Dad, it's just that..."

"Quiet, girl. I'm talking to the boys. Are you playing cowboys?"

Senhor Tuarles's eyes were bloodshot, his mouth was mildly swollen. It was obvious that this wasn't just from the beers that he liked to drink, even if it was after lunch; the heat at that time of day made a person's body feel limp and swollen. We children didn't feel this because we were always running.

"No, Senhor Tuarles, we just came for that can."

"That can? A can of what?"

"It's just a joke, Dad."

"Quiet, daughter. Go inside and we'll talk later. Are you playing in the street at this hour with the sun on your head?"

"We were just about to go look for hats, Senhor Tuarles," I tried.

"You were going to look for hats in Granma Maria's chicken coop?"

"No, Senhor Tuarles, we came here to the chicken coop to look for paint thinner."

"Ah, so on top of everything else you're playing with paint thinner after lunch?"

"Senhor Tuarles." 3.14 was pretty gutsy at times. "If you prefer, we could only play with the paint thinner in the late afternoon."

"Are you getting off on that shit or what?" Senhor Tuarles never had any trouble saying the craziest stuff and everybody knew that he had an AK-47 at home.

"No, Senhor Tuarles, we were just on a mission, like, eh."

"'Like, eh'? What kind of Portuguese are they teaching you at that school? Huh?"

"Sorry, Senhor Tuarles."

"It looks like what you boys are in need of is a good thrashing...Isn't that it?" His body stirred very slowly, as though his head were playing that tango from the military hospital. "Gimme that can, I'll take care of the paint thinner."

"But, Senhor Tuarles..."

"Do you want to be disobedient at this hour, in this heat? Hand me the comrade paint thinner. And not a peep, or I'll go get my AK-47... Scat, the both of you!"

We fled. He stood laughing; but you never knew, at that time of day, with his body stumbling in a kind of slow dance and his eyes really red, whether he might not go get the AK-47 just to prove that he was telling the truth.

Without the paint thinner, we sat down on the sidewalk in front of Senhor Tuarles's house and looked at the Comrade Gas Jockey, who was about to fall out of his chair from a long bout of failing to stay awake.

In Granma Nhé's yard the parrots started to talk nonsense again. "Son of a snorer and a nuzzler"; the other shouted more loudly, "You're an etcetera": all in soap opera voices. Then we went into the old chicken coop and peeped out: there was Comrade Gudafterov hurrying out of the kitchen with bags of food in his hands, and the only person who was in the house was Madalena Kamussekele.

"What's in those bags?"

"They look like leftovers."

"But do you guys have a stock of leftovers, or what?"

"What do you mean?"

"Wow—the leftovers at your granma's house last forever. Even Gudafterov's taking some."

"There must be a tale here. We're going to ask Madalena."

"And if she tells on us?"

"She's going to tell on us? We're the ones who can tell. The leftovers belong to my granma."

When Comrade Gudafterov had left, we went around the corner and found Madalena in the kitchen still tidying up the leftovers of the leftovers.

"Didn't I tell you?" 3.14 laughed. "Here in your house left-overs are provisions. We should tell FAPLA, hahaha!"

"What are you guys doin' here?" Madalena was startled.

"We're on a reconnaissance mission." 3.14 crossed his arms. He looked like a sheriff in the movies.

"You're what?"

"It's not worth it, Madalena, we caught you. We saw Comrade Gudafterov leaving here with bags of food."

"He came to ask. He said he was hungry."

"That's a lie, Comrade Madalena, the Soviets are never hungry. At most, they're thirsty."

"He said he needed food."

"What for?"

"He said it was a 'secret.'"

"And what 'secret' is that?"

"He always comes here for food on Thursdays. But I don't know what it's for."

"Good food?"

"No, just leftovers."

"It must be for the birds in the storage shed," 3.14 said to me in secret.

"Just don't tell on me to Granma, or I'll get another thrashing."

"We're not going to tell on you, but don't forget: we never asked you for the wire cutters."

We went outside again, which is what we should have done in the first place to follow Gudafterov to see where he was going.

"Do you figure it's for those birds?"

"It must be."

"And what are those birds for?"

"Could be that they eat birds. They say that the Chinese eat dogs, and in Cabinda Province they eat monkeys."

"Is that so?"

"Yeah."

Lots of trucks had started to roll off the construction site, full of garbage and sand that wasn't going to be used. The late afternoon dust of Bishop's Beach got stirred up again. Dona Libânia came to the window with the cloth handkerchief that she put over her nose. The Comrade Gas Jockey also covered his face and blinked his eyes, and if Granma Nhé had been there, with all those dust clouds, she would have ordered me back into the house because of my asthma attacks. And then I remembered her in the operating room.

"Do you think it sucks having a toe cut off?"

"To tell you the truth, if it's done with an anaesthetic, I figure it shouldn't be too much of a hassle. But if they don't have any anaesthetics in the military hospital, it must hurt like anything."

"I guess Comrade Rafael KnockKnock wouldn't do that to her. And Aunty Tó wouldn't let him."

"You're right. It's not going to hurt at all. It's just when she wakes up that she might feel some pain."

The dust lifted in spirals like the smoke from mountains dynamited in cowboy movies. The trucks passed by, the drivers shouted words in Soviet, Sea Foam bounced around, running with his threads and his dreads dancing in the wind, and the drivers honked their horns to avoid running him over.

"Hey, listen." 3.14 was also fanning his face to keep the dust away. "Is it really true that Rafael KnockKnock put on a tango so that your aunt would dance with him?"

"I swear it's true. I was there and I saw it."

"That guy must be a bit crazy, too. He doesn't even know how to speak Angolan."

"I think he did it so that she'd be happy before the operation. Maybe it helps. I dunno... I started wondering if she isn't going to miss her toe. My granma's very conceited."

"I doubt it. That's just the granmas gossiping. Also, she has so many other digits, how's she going to miss one of them?"

"Yeah, you're right."

"But listen, that tango music, is it Cuban?"

"It must be."

"And how come he couldn't just put on a *kizomba*?"

"I guess you can't dance a *kizomba* with a crippled toe."

Often, when I saw Sea Foam come running, I'd start laughing.

"You goin' crazy, too?" 3.14 would ask me.

I laughed a little less hard. Sometimes I kept my feelings secret; other times I didn't, I spoke the truth.

"Sea Foam looks like a bird that's about to take off."

And so he did. I dreamed about this once: his feet coming closer and closer to not touching the ground, his threads taking on the shape of a MiG's wings, his dreads standing out straight to indicate the direction of his flight, his feet peddling in the air, and he himself laughing at me, uttering phrases in the crazed Cuban that he spoke.

I saw him come running from the bakery, down that alley we used to go to the Kinanga Cinema, and he accelerated fast. Maybe when he was studying in Cuba he was also one of those athletes: it seems like sports is a duty over there and they wake up early to go swimming or running. I don't know; that's what I've heard. Foam always wanted to run a race against João Serrador's 1100 motorcycle, but he didn't last, the bike went past him faster than a cannon ball. João Serrador only braked when he was already close to the curve, and if he pulled a wheelie—which he did a lot—the stop was even more abrupt and we applauded him, and right there Foam discarded everything he had in his hands to leap up and applaud João Serrador's manoeuvres.

That morning I saw Foam running in a silence where the only noise was made by his feet hitting the ground. I remembered again the near take-off he failed to achieve because he was carrying an enormous sheaf of newspapers in his arms. The papers made you think of the Delta wings that used to appear during the breaks on television.

He was running very fast in our direction.

"Let's just split," 3.14 requested. "Don't you see he's coming this way?" He grabbed my hand to pull me.

"Why should we run? He never did a thing to you."

"He's got a screw loose. Some day he might think I am an American ship and want to bombard me. Didn't you hear about that idea of his about finding clues to an American invasion and I don't know what else?"

"Cool it. He knows you're Pi, better known in Angola and the far-away Soviet Union as Comrade 3.14. Hahaha!"

"Are you making fun of me? If he attacks you, don't wait for me to save you. I'll even tell him to bombard you with napalm, like in the Vietnam movies."

"Cool it, man. He's not in that kind of mood."

"How do you know?"

"Just look at his face. He wants to talk to somebody."

Sea Foam looked just like João Serrador's bike. He hit the brakes when he got close to us, and even kicked up dust.

"The plans, *compañeros. El futuro* is close, a de-fence against *el pasado*."

"A fence?"

"Closer." He lowered the newspaper, spreading it over the ground like a big map. "Not a single tiny house will remain!"

It was a huge page with a half-crumpled drawing of the government's plan for the whole Mausoleum area, with tiny pictures that were dotted with symbols where they were going to put new parks, swing sets, a new waterfront drive close to the sea, lots of space with lawns where dogs could walk and poop all over, slides, water fountains, mature trees that I don't know how they were going to grow so fast, and a ton of people lining up to enter the Mausoleum and see the body of the Comrade President, embalmed with Soviet techniques.

"Whoa. Wait a minute." 3.14 looked really frightened. "I don't see my house here—or even the gas station."

"I don't see the beach with the Old Fisherman's boat, or my granma's house, either."

"And I don't see the kennel I have in my yard to keep a certain animal... Hahaha." Sea Foam said "animal" with a crazy voice and we took off running to get away from him.

"Didn't I warn you?" As 3.14 ran, he looked as if he'd seen a soap opera wolfman.

"Just keep running and don't look back."

"Right now is when we're gonna get bombarded."

Foam loved to frighten children. He had never once touched anybody; maybe one time somebody had fallen over fleeing from him because a person who's running can slip and hit a knee on a stone, blood can even flow, but it was never on purpose. Except once Senhor Tuarles grabbed Foam and, to be on the safe side, unloaded one hell of a thrashing on him just to calm him down for a while.

Foam grabbed the sheaf of newspapers again and almost took off flying. He ran without looking at the car that was about to pass, crossed the square, hit the edge of the beach running flat out and, wetting his feet and his clothes, only stopped to talk to the Old Fisherman, way off in the distance.

"We can stop. His missiles aren't long-range." 3.14 was sweating like anything.

"Could all that stuff be for real?"

"You think the *Jornal de Angola* is going to print lies? You retard—everything that comes out in the *Jornal de Angola* is the truth—the Comrade President authorized them to come out there."

"So that's the new Bishop's Beach?"

"Naw...That's a dream." 3.14 looked at me with the face of a madman.

"How so?"

"Our plan, don't you remember? That page just had a drawing, as if it were the description of a wish. I mean, since you can't really write about a wish, they drew a picture."

"You're talking bullshit, Pi."

"No, you're the one who's not getting it. That's how come I always say our plan has to go ahead."

"We'll never do it."

"Don't say that, Comrade. The struggle continues." He laughed.

"Victory is certain. Yeah, I know."

"I'm serious. You saw the dynamite."

"Be serious, Pi. We can't go messing around with that dynamite. If we do we'll just die without having grown up to be elders."

"You're being thick because dynamite only goes off if you ignite it. First, you gotta set it right, then you've gotta connect up the wick. Only then can you light it."

"And if they catch us? What if we go to jail at this age? Or if they send us to the front lines to fight South African japies?"

"First, only people who are over sixteen years old or whatever are sent to the front lines. Second, kids our age aren't allowed in jails."

"How do you know?"

"Third, nobody here's going to tell on us. Unless it's Charlita. But also, who's even going to believe that the two of us were the ones who dexploded a Mausoleum, that size, guarded by a bunch of lobsters that blue?"

I knew that when it was time to act, 3.14 lost all fear. I had already gone with him to a bonfire that had been forgotten on the beach. We took real AK-47 bullets with us, from a soldier who wanted cigarettes in exchange, and when it was time to throw the bullets into the bonfire I said that we better not do it.

“Then keep yours. I’m throwing my bullets into the fire.”

“What if they shoot back at us?”

“Don’t be a scaredy-cat. You think with so many directions they’re going to choose to come right at our legs to get us back?”

Before I could utter a word in reply, he laughed as if he were eating the world’s best baobab ice cream, threw the bullets high into the air towards the middle of the bonfire and took off running. I went after him. We didn’t look back, but it appeared that the bullets had stayed there, heating up in the fire. We ran skidding with all the strength of our legs’ sweat, and when we rounded the trunk of that fat palm tree we heard two high-pitched shot-like reports and the sound of tin being pierced. One bullet had gone who-knows-where, while the other had pierced the can that was next to us.

“You see! The bullet chose the can because it makes more noise than our legs. Hahaha!” 3.14 looked back at the fire and tried to persuade me to throw my bullets, too, but I wasn’t brave enough.

“I’m going to hold onto them. If some day there’s a home invasion at my granma’s house, at least I have two bullets.”

3.14 could have given me a ribbing over that line about keeping bullets without even having an AK-47 in the house to shoot with, but he didn’t say anything. He laid a hand on my shoulder and we stayed there warming our faces in front of the yellow fire that smelled of the dust of cunning bullets that liked to pierce cans rather than the legs of Bishop’s Beach’s children.

“What you thinkin’ about?”

“I’m not thinking, I’m remembering.”

“What are you remembering?”

“Nothing, leave it.” I pointed at Comrade Rafael Knock-Knock’s Lada. “Look who’s coming.”

“Your granma with nineteen fingers and toes!” he shouted in delight.

I hadn’t even known you could fit that many people into one of those old Ladas. Doctor Rafael was driving, Granma

Nhé was in the front seat; behind them was Aunty Tó, her husband, my mother, a nurse and even Madalena Kamussekele, laughing with her head out the window.

They went around the square, on the far side of the gas pump. The Comrade Gas Jockey waved goodbye the way that he always did, in spite of the fact that people lived nearby. I don't know; everybody has the right to use up as many goodbyes as he wants, but I figure that waving goodbye is something you do more for a departure of the long-trip type, like when somebody goes in an airplane to some other international country, or even to another province, as long as they stay there for more than two weeks, or you wave goodbye when you're so far away that your voice doesn't reach even if you shout so loudly that your throat hurts, or if it's like in those movies about big ships that sometimes sink, then it's worth going down to the port to wave goodbye, with or without a handkerchief, with or without tears. There are even people who like to wave goodbye while laughing and keeping their longing to cry hidden, because the person who's leaving is already sad to be going so far away, and they don't need to take the tears from our prolonged goodbye with them; and then, if it's a person who likes the person who's leaving a lot, and they're going away, even if it's only for a few days, then maybe it's all right to give them a little goodbye wave, but not so extravagantly that you're almost imitating the Comrade Traffic Cop like the Comrade Gas Jockey does. On top of that, I should say that you never wave a very big goodbye to a person who's coming home, but it's not worth explaining more. A lot of elders don't understand a thing about waving goodbye.

The car stopped and we reached it at the same time as the dust that always arrives a little bit late, just like Madalena Kamussekele. It's useless making any kind of appointment with her, even to watch a soap opera or a movie at the Kinanga Cinema—she's going to arrive late. It seems that one time my cousin Nitó, who's also known as Sankara, hit her for this. I mean, everybody was waiting for the afternoon matinée that started at three o'clock, and Madalena, just because she was on course to arrive five minutes early, stopped at the final bend to wait for a moment and ask a passing elder for the time—just to be certain that she arrived late. Nitó boxed her ears a couple of times to make her lose this habit, though she still hasn't lost it to this day.

Granma Nhé's eyes looked tired, and a little swollen, too, and on her arm I saw those little stains from when someone gives blood, the skin all purple and looking like it hurts like anything.

"Granma. We were here waiting for Granma." 3.14 laughed as he spoke and looked into the car to try to find the spot where the toe no longer was.

"What 'Granma' is that?" I gave him a nudge and pulled him out of the way. "Is this the confidence you picked up in the Mausoleum, or what? Is your granma around here?"

"Cool it. Granmas are loaned out here on Bishop's Beach."

"There's nothing to loan here. Everybody fixes himself up with his own granma. And anyways, mine's awesome and she only has nineteen digits."

Granma Nhé laughed. At last she seemed to be in a good mood.

Comrade Rafael KnockKnock went around the front of the car and succeeded in opening Granma Nhé's door without saying "KnockKnock." It was a miracle of forgetting.

"Oh, no, *un momentito*," he said, while he shooed us away. "I forgot *por completo*."

He closed the door again, so that we all burst out laughing in disbelief: he regarded Granma Nhé with a clownish face, and said in a loud voice: "KnockKnock. Now, *sí, abuela*." Granma was laughing so hard that she almost wasn't able to stand up.

"*Me gusta* seeing you like that, *Abuela*. What a joyous heart you have, what a marvellous smile!"

The foot emerged all wrapped up in some gauze that didn't allow you to see anything from any operation.

"You okay, Granma?"

"Yes, my dear. Give me a kiss on the cheek."

"How many toes did they cut off?"

"Only one, *compañero*."

"*Mucho bien*," 3.14 said. Nobody expected that; we all laughed again. Granma asked that nobody make any more jokes because shaking with laughter made her foot ache.

The elders went to the living room to speak with the nurse and Madalena was sent to the kitchen because she had stood there listening to the elders' conversations.

3.14 and I pretended to stay on the veranda to play a game, but we were paying attention to what they were saying because Aunty Tó had the *Jornal de Angola* in her hand, and it looked like they were also going to talk about the drawing that Pi had called a description of a wish.

"We can't wait much longer, we have to think about Mother's future, where we're going to put—"

We caught isolated phrases and it was only by pasting them together in our imagination that we understood the worries that they were discussing.

"Poor Dona Agnette. She's lived here almost her whole life."

"Her and all of these people. It's going to be a problem."

Which meant that nobody was talking about the children. It was all very well that our lives were still so short, but we also liked Bishop's Beach a lot, and the elders always forget that when there are problems we can help to solve them.

"It's just that they never include us when they talk about stuff."

"We're going to solve this, don't worry." Once again, 3.14 spoke in that serious way of his that made it sound as if he was at a political rally.

"But do you know how much dynamite they have there?"

"They have enough to blow up all the houses on Bishop's Beach. I figure that amount's enough for our plan. As long as nobody tells on us." He glanced at me.

"You ever seen me tell on anybody?" I asked in a low voice.

"Have I ever seen you tell?" he laughed. "Every time we eat green mangoes with salt you end up telling your granma."

"That's different. She asks me how come I've got diarrhea and I can't lie to her."

"Just be ready." He got up, tightened his belt, hitched up his trousers; he looked like a cowboy getting ready for the last shoot-out of his life. "This time you're going to have to lie, even if they say they're going to give you a beating."

3.14 was speaking seriously. He got up on the low wall of the veranda and motioned for me to climb up as well.

From up there we could see almost all of Bishop's Beach: on the left-hand side, the construction site of the Mausoleum, a few distant houses, Dona Libânia's house, the gas pump; off in the distance, the house on the bend before the pretty church, the green houses, Sea Foam's house, Paulinha's house, Aunt Adelaide's house; then right nearby, almost attached, Senhor Tuarles's enormous house with his five daughters, of whom only Charlita had good glasses, the same house that had the old chicken coop where so many games were played and the smell of Granma Maria's *kitaba*, with or without chili pepper, then the house of Gadinho, who wasn't allowed to play with us, and beyond that, where we could no longer see, other houses: the house of Paulinho, who took judo classes and helped his father, and behind it the house of André, who was a commando and already had killed a ton of South African japies, and only now and then received authorization to come back and visit his family. War must not be anything like it is in the movies because when André comes home he's hungry and so sad that he can't speak a word; he cries when the truck comes to pick him up again and take him to some war zone. On the other side of the street was the bakery where, before five AM, people go to put their stones in the line-up that everybody respects, and right beside it is the alley where we play in our good clothes on Carnival of Victory Day with the whistle that Granma Catarina lends us; that alley is the muddy street that leads to the Kinanga Cinema, where they show ninja movies, and movies about Godzilla with his enormous mouth, about Trinità, about the Gendarmes and Gendarmettes of Saint-Tropez, and even the most delicious movie in the world, called *The Big Brawl*, with Jackie Chan and his uncle who fights like anything. After the Kinanga Cinema we could turn the corner and find the back of the church, where one time Senhor Tuarles had to go and beat the shit out of the priest who was being a pervert with the little girls of Bishop's Beach; Senhor Tuarles sent Dona Isabel to go get his AK-47, but in the end he didn't use it and just beat up the priest instead of killing him, and we were all up on top of the wall—yes, without that whole life that the elders had already lived but that we knew through the tales that we had seen and invented, as well as those that were told, retold or improved by Sea Foam, with his seashell-strung dreadlocks, stories of Kianda, who is also a mermaid, who the Old Fisherman says he saw but others say he couldn't have seen, Granma Maria's tales in Kimbundu, of which we never understood a word, not even today, because at school they never taught us to speak or write Kimbundu, tales told by the Comrade Gas Jockey when he drank and talked too much, tales told by Senhor Tuarles, who spoke little but also had charming tales about the old days, tales of Granma Catarina, who opened and closed windows; and lots of people go around saying that we, the children, are talking hogwash, that she no longer lives in the house of my Granma Nhé, who we now call Granma Nineteen: tales of Bishop's Beach in the time of the tugas, with less dust than now, and it seems that people talked differently but also, after all, the country was under occupation and lacking any real independence, and, beyond that, so that you won't say that I forgot about them, all of the tales that Granma Nineteen tells me; so many of them, with so many names, so many people and clothing styles, with dances and pianos and Fado music and trips and love affairs, with chats and thoughts and tenderness, and the silent pauses that are part of the tales that she tells me after lunch—and all that, at times, so often, I don't know why, makes the elders think that we're not going to remember everything, one day when we look back and think about our dusty Bishop's Beach.

"Be ready." 3.14 spoke gently, with his eyes nearly moist, and it wasn't from the dust. "From this time onwards you're going to have to lie when they ask you if we were the people who dexploded the Mausoleum construction site."

The wind made a cute sound as it passed in a flying curve through the trees of Granma Nineteen's yard: the old fig tree, the guava tree, the mango tree, the cherimoya tree, the bushes, the papaya tree, the red Brazilian cherry tree.

"I know, Pi, I know."

After lunch Comrade Gudafterov arrived, drenched in sweat and reeking of body odour. He didn't know it, but Granma Nineteen preferred him to visit at night, after 6PM, when he had taken his bath and washed his armpits, because if there's one way to know that Comrade Gudafterov is near, that way is called Soviet Body Odour. Or simply "b.o.-dorov," as Comrade 3.14 used to say.

"Kildren, you just play? Look at marvellous construction of Mausoleum. Very pretty, like big rocket, very pretty!"

"You're gonna see that big rocket take off," 3.14 said. His teeth were jammed tight together, but I understood him.

"Gudafterov no understand."

"Just wait, Goofofferov, you're gonna understand."

"Kildren, Granma Nhéte come back good?"

"Yeah, she came back."

"Gudafterov want greet her."

3.14 jumped off the wall from above the bushes, almost crippling himself. He burst out laughing and I knew he was going to say something.

"Gudafterov! Go wash your armpitovs! Hahaha!"

"Granma Nhéte is wake up?"

"Has she woken up?"

"Yes, woken up."

"I don't know, Comrade Gudafterov. You'd better go ask the elders."

"Gudafteroooov!" 3.14 shouted, making a megaphone of his hands. Sea Foam laughed so hard he rolled around on the sand; the Comrade Gas Jockey was guffawing. "Gudafterooov, we don't like b.o.-dorov! Go wash your armpitovs!"

The sun warmed my face and my laughter and the things and the names and the houses, and all the people of Bishop's Beach refused to leave my imagination. As hard as I tried to stop them, a slew of voices spoke at once: some laughed, others cried, the children made noise as they ran around, Sea Foam took flight holding aloft a sheet of newsprint, the Old Fisherman appeared with Rainboat repainted a bright new shade of blue, and from Granma Nineteen's house to the sea was a heap of sand that had never known the cement of the Mausoleum construction site.

I opened my eyes.

For the first time, I thought about 3.14's plan without my heart accelerating with fear at having to lie about things which, after all, we just had to get done.

Comrade Gudafterov came out with a disconsolate expression on his face and made no jokes in his Soviet-accented Angolan Portuguese. He said goodbye to me just as he was about to go out the front gate and ran his hands through the flowers at the entrance as though bidding them farewell. On top of everything else, Granma Nineteen didn't like people messing around with her flowers as if they were patting a dog. But Granma didn't see him; she only came downstairs later.

On the top floor, after looking out at us, Granma Catarina closed the windows for the last time that day.

"Are you thinking about life, son?" Granma Nineteen liked to say that she didn't sleep at night in order to concentrate on "thinking about life."

"I'm just lookin' at our Bishop's Beach. Did Gudafterov bring bad news, Granma? It was even in the *Jornal de Angola.*"

"The comrade's name is Bilhardov."

"Bilhardov, Gudafterov, Armpitov. He's been given so many names here, Granma, that when he returns to his country he won't know what he's called."

Granma Nineteen moaned with pain from her bandaged foot, but she still laughed.

"Do you want me to get you a chair?"

"No, it's good to walk. It just hurts."

"Do you miss your toe, Granma?"

"No. Everything's fine, son." She also looked at our Bishop's Beach, with the sea behind it showing off the shade of blue that they call navy. "Everything's fine."

"Granma, they're going to dexplode all the houses, eh?"

"It's 'explode,' son. Don't talk like that; people will think you don't know how to speak Portuguese."

"I like 'dexplode' better. It's a word that sounds like it's bursting open; explode seems like it should be for a slow flame."

"All right, but only say those invented words of yours in the house."

"Bilhardov came to tell you, eh?"

"Yes, he came. Tomorrow they're going to close the beach. Orders from one of those generals who commands the construction site."

"So it's already starting."

"Yes, it's already starting."

Granma asked me to go and see if there was water in the faucet.

She knew very well that there was no water at that hour, but to please her I turned on the faucet to see, turned it off again, re-arranged the hose that had already been arranged, just to do something, to allow her time to see if she wanted to tell me about their conversation. But she didn't say a word.

"If I were feeling better, I'd water the plants just like that."

"With make-believe water, Granma? I think you should only do that in the house, otherwise people are going to think you've lost your mind."

"Watering does the plants good, but it also does good to the person who waters. Even with make-believe water, as you say."

Granma went back inside without saying anything more. She didn't even tell me what time dinner was, or that I couldn't go and play with the other kids in the square.

The sun had gone away, the Comrade Gas Jockey wasn't there anymore and 3.14 had already whistled twice.

We sat down on Senhor Tuarles's sidewalk to wait for Charlita. We thought she might have been punished, but she showed up.

"Charlita, you never showed up again. Are you sick, or what?"

"My dad keeps telling me not to go out into the street because any minute now they're going to start dynamiting the houses."

"That's not how it works. They have to warn people first. They're going to close the beach and order everybody out. Each person can only take one chair and a bag with their underwear. Not even toothbrushes are allowed, that's what I heard."

"You're full of it." 3.14 knew this was a lie.

"I'm just kiddin', but it's true, they're going to close the beach."

"How do you close a beach? With a padlock?"

"You just put men with guns there."

"They've had them on the beach forever."

"But they never actually stopped you from going there. They already know us. Now they're not going to let us play there anymore."

"And Foam? And the Old Fisherman? Are they gonna take his dugout to his new house?"

"What do I know?"

"Charlita?"

"What is it?"

"It's just that you're so quiet. Our plan's really advanced."

"I don't want to hear any more about that crazy plan. My dad was already set to give me a thrashing because of it." Charlita scratched at the ground with a stone, making some very ugly drawings.

"Your dad? Don't tell me you already tattled on us."

"It's not that. He was suspicious. It seems he heard our conversation, and he came to warn me that he didn't want to hear anything about dynamite or playing jokes on the Soviets."

"It's not a joke."

"That's what I told him. He bawled me out and told me not to play with you guys any more. He said you were boys and you play dangerous games like putting AK-47 bullets in a bonfire."

"We only did that once."

"Three times." 3.14 corrected me.

"I told him that, too, but he still doesn't want me to."

"Does he know about the plan?"

"He had drunk a lot, but he knows we went there and saw the dynamite."

"Is he gonna tell my granma?"

"I don't think so. He was weird."

"Weird, how?"

"It was like a message."

"A message?"

"For you guys."

"What do you mean?"

"He said you should be careful because you can't light dynamite with a normal match."

"Is that right?"

"Yup. And it has to be buried."

"Is it possible he wants to participate in our plan, 3.14?"

"I doubt it."

"Sometimes elders aren't brave enough to speak up."

"I've gotta go back inside. I can't stay out here with you guys. He's already watchin' me from the window."

"But why did you tell him, Charlita?"

"He threatened to take away my glasses when the soap opera came on, and if I didn't tell him he wouldn't take me to Portugal on a trip to get my sight fixed."

"All right, go inside. If we need something, can we still ask you?"

"I guess it's better if I don't know anything else. Good luck and take care."

"Charlita." 3.14 got up to whisper in her ear. "You don't know anything but it's going to be tomorrow night."

"Okay, I don't know anything."

Dark as the street was, we were amazed that the mosquitoes weren't there to sting our legs. We didn't need to fan ourselves or to watch out; the sea breeze or the smoke from some bonfire must have driven away the mosquitoes to go nail legs in some other neighbourhood.

Some stars began to appear in the sky, but there were only a few of them and they shone with a muted gleam.

"Sea Foam says that if there weren't any stars shining up there, the sky wouldn't move at all; it would be a place we looked at without seeing any beauty."

"I don't think that's what he said."

"More or less. He spouts a lot of nonsense, too, when he's talking to himself."

"But he spouts nonsense in Cuban while we only spout nonsense in Angolan."

We ran our hands over our legs out of habit, in an attempt not to be bitten, because, aside from the fever and vomiting, malaria always left us without the strength or energy to play for almost five days, so we had to avoid it.

"Listen, talking of spouting nonsense...You know what I was thinking last night when I couldn't sleep?"

"What?"

"When I grow up I'm gonna have a pile of money from a business that I already invented just for me." 3.14 laughed.

"What's that?"

"You can't tell anybody."

"Okay, just say it."

"I'm going to be the owner of trucks that settle the dust in the neighbourhoods."

"A great idea."

"Have you ever thought about it? There must be a heap of neighbourhoods here in Luanda where it's dusty in the late afternoon. I'm going to become rich overnight."

"And what are you going to do with the money?"

"I figure I'm going to give it to my poor old dad. He never has money. They pay him really badly at the Mausoleum construction site."

"You're doing the right thing. If I had piles of money I'd buy a really big garden."

"What for?"

"To plant mango trees, guava trees and avocados."

"What for?"

"Here we're always waitin' for the fruit to ripen on the trees. There, since there'd be lots of them, one of them would always have fruit that was ripe. We'd always have plenty of mangoes and guavas."

"Good idea."

"And one more thing...The trees would be full of bats and we'd be able to kill them with my cousin's pellet gun."

"And would you invite me along?"

"Of course. I'd buy a ton of trees that would have a ton of bats."

"It's a deal. You invite me and give me a brand-spanking new pellet gun. I give you a dust-settling truck."

"You've got a deal. Later, when you're an elder, it won't be any use sayin' that you've forgotten this conversation we had here today, long before we became adults."

"Cool it. I'm not going to forget."

Before I had time to finish my breakfast in peace, Granma Nineteen herself sent me to go and see what was causing all of the screaming out there on the beach.

I set off at a run and saw other children running, too. From far off, I recognized Sea Foam's dreadlocks, the hunched body of the Old Fisherman, and other Bishop's Beach elders, Russian soldiers with reddened faces—all arguing at the same time. Suddenly a shot from an AK-47 rang out; two shots, as a matter of fact. But we barely ducked, the elders weren't scared and, from far away, Senhor Tuarles gestured to Dona Isabel, his wife, to get his AK-47, which he kept under the bed in his room.

The sun, as always, took no prisoners, and people had to squint their eyes or even hold a hand over them, as though it were the brim of a hat, to see the person they were arguing with. That was the remedy that made it possible to see, but by now nobody was hearing anything; they were just griping, which is the manner of a person who just shouts without knowing whether anybody's getting the message.

Soviet soldiers, known in Luanda as "blue ants," and later baptized "blue lobsters" on Bishop's Beach, had new placards forbidding everyone from using the beach and approaching the water, which had pretty white foam and occasionally, in the month of August, a few jellyfish whose burning stings wore off only when the bite was rubbed with hot sand. And nobody wanted to give in.

Comrade Gudafterov looked as if it hurt him to carry out the orders he'd been given. He gesticulated without much conviction and concentrated as though he were listening when the Old Fisherman spoke to him. Many voices spoke at the same time; off in the distance, people stayed on their verandas or at their windows watching that fracas on the sands of the ocean.

Later, a car also arrived full of police, who watched from a distance, as though the fracas was between the blue lobsters and the residents of Bishop's Beach.

"But us guys are here with just a little scrap of beach made from the white hairs of the sea," Sea Foam was shouting, "we never went to Russia or the Soviet Union to close or open or inaugurate or invade a Soviet beach...But you, misguided reptiles..."

"You comrades think you're just closing a beach—but who's gonna give food to our children tomorrow?" shouted the comrade wife of another fisherman whose whole family's names I've forgotten.

"Comrades, superior orders from Comrade Boss General, we just follow order, not decide put forbid placard." Gudafterov couldn't even explain things clearly.

"We know very well what you're going to do next, but we're not idiots here and we won't let you. Get away from this beach, nobody owns it. Kianda herself will punish you in your illegal fishing boats, you fucking tupariovs!" Senhor Tuarles was shouting, but now he was gesturing to Dona Isabel not to bring the AK-47 because the police were there to see who was the biggest troublemaker. Fortunately, everybody was being disorderly together, and no one stood out as the person who should be arrested.

I saw that instead of looking in the direction of the ruckus, 3.14 was observing the rest of Bishop's Beach. I even thought he was searching for someone, but later he looked for a long time at the edges of the fence where there was the hole that we used to get in whenever we wanted to. He came to talk to me.

"We're going to take a chance now because this uproar is going to last for a long time. I'm seein' more fishermen comin' and in a moment the police are gonna start firing."

"What are you talkin' about?"

"Distraction manoeuvres. Don't you remember?"

"Weren't they diversion manoeuvres?"

"But where's the diversion if this business is serious? The important thing is that we've got to take advantage of this opportunity. Come on."

"Should I call Charlita?"

"No. Her dad will just come and wreck everything. We're going to leave unexpectedly."

"Leave how?"

"Leave unexpectedly."

"I don't get it. What's going on?"

"You're so slow. It's leaving without anybody seeing us, unexpectedly, when nobody expected we were going to leave, retreat-style."

"And where do we go?"

"Into enemy territory."

"Now?"

"Let's just go. They're all here, I already checked. Look, over there on the left-hand side, arguing with the lady-elder, that's Dimitry, which means that nobody's guarding the storage shed."

"Won't it be locked up?"

"Of course not. At this time of day, Gudafterov-Armpitov will have already opened it so that they can take out the materials."

We lowered our heads a little, hoping no one was going to see us. Sea Foam winked and grabbed Comrade Gudafterov's shoulder when he was about to turn in our direction. We pretended that we were heading towards the houses and had barely reached Dona Libânia's wall when we entered the alley that led to the back of the Mausoleum construction site.

3.14 was right: everything was empty, open, the machinery abandoned, shovels and picks lying on the ground, even an open toolbox where we went to rip off a brand-new pair of wire cutters.

"You never know when you might need them," 3.14 said in a serious voice.

"You figure we got time?"

"At least to start. You ready?"

"For what?"

"We're gonna place the dynamite."

"Place it where?"

"In the spots we judge to be the best."

"And how are we gonna know that?"

"Are you touched? How long have we known our way around this construction site?"

"Since we were born."

"Then it's just a question of choosing. Remember that this is a big circle and everything depends on the quantity of dynamite. All we have to do is set it right, spread it around, and that's all it takes for the old cowboy to go west, as they say in the movies."

"I don't know if the dynamite is powerful enough to break up all this cement, Pi."

"Don't start making things up. If cowboys can dynamite mountains, how can a Mausoleum built by drunken Soviets not go flying? Just remember the cardinal points we studied in school."

"What for?"

"I already thought about it. I already divided everything up: your granma's house there is the north."

"So what?"

"We're going to divide everything into eight sections. I get the north, the south, the east and the west."

"How come I get the others?"

"Because I don't remember the other points' names."

"I figure it was... Northeast... Northwest... Souteast..."

"Souteast or southeast?"

"Maybe southeast. And then another one I don't remember..."

"It doesn't matter. Wherever there's a gap, you put one. Now let's go."

There was a watchtower, I mean there were two of them, but only one oversaw the storage shed and had a Soviet guard, who was always very seated and asleep.

"You figure he's asleep?"

"Let's just go. If they catch us, we say that we came to give back these wire cutters."

We ran towards the storage shed, which wasn't actually as small as it had seemed. It had closets with many shelves and smelled strongly of food and birdshit. When we entered we had to close the door; we stood in a darkness that was almost frightening because the birds started to make noise, and that scared us a little.

"Jeeze! I can't see anything," 3.14 said in a frightened voice. "I'm probably gonna slip on some grenade."

"You figure they got grenades in here?"

"I don't know. They say Soviets are crazy about keeping grenades under their pillows."

"You're always making stuff up."

"I'm not making it up; they do that in war zones. That way when they run out of bullets they can still throw a grenade that kills at least five people."

"Five? I think you're exaggerating."

"It doesn't matter, don't move. We're just gonna wait for the birds to quiet down and make sure the watchman in the tower hasn't heard anything. Don't you have matches with you?"

"You want me to light matches in a room full of dynamite?"

"Didn't Senhor Tuarles say dynamite couldn't be lit with a normal match?"

"Who's saying my matches are normal? What if they're abnormal, or 'unexpected,' as you say?"

"But do you have some or not?"

"Of course I don't have any! I don't walk around every morning with a box of matches in my pocket."

"You could have got some. You knew the mission was going to take place at any moment."

"We'd agreed it was going to happen at night."

"But the world is full of surprises, Comrade, and we have to take advantage of them. So how are we going to see?"

"We'll just wait a little."

"What for?"

"We'll just wait a little. Our eyes are going to get used to it, you're going to start seeing in the darkness."

"See in the darkness? I've never done that."

"But you're going to now. The darkness is like a joke: it's over quickly."

And soon it happened. He even gave a laugh of amazement. "You're right."

Of course it wasn't seeing with the beautiful clarity of perceiving the differences between the pretty colours on the crests of those dumb birds that were all crammed in together, tons of them, in pretty cages that seemed to be made of a wicker-like material, perhaps to make them look like fishing baskets in the river that we had studied at school. The poor birds were crammed together, big ones mixed with small ones, the short-billed with the long-billed, some that seemed to fly a lot with others that only liked to fly a little. In the dim light it wasn't even possible to tell which was which; all we could see with absolute certainty was that, in other cages, there were much bigger, much prettier parrots than Just Parrot and His Name.

The birds were such good friends to us that they all shut up and we stood listening to each other's breathing and to the tiny noises that their claws made in the papers at the bottom of each cage.

"Poor little things, all alone here in the darkness."

"The problem is, they can't fly."

"Look at the boxes."

By luck, the dynamite was all on the two lower shelves, where we were able to get at it. If the boxes with their danger signs, with death's-heads and fire symbols, had been higher up, they would have been more difficult to reach. The words were all in Russian, or even Soviet, I'm not sure which.

"Are you going to open it?"

"Yeah."

"You're not afraid?"

"Afraid of what?"

"That it's booby-trapped?"

"Is a box of dynamite going to be booby-trapped? You've watched too many shoot-'em-up movies."

It was just like in the movies: long, russet-coloured bars, with a little thread at the end where you lighted it.

"How many can you carry?"

"Let me see how much they weigh."

They weren't heavy and, in fact, were thinner than they looked.

"Four for each of them?"

"There are going to be eight holes. We can put two in each hole."

"Okay."

Each of us stuck four pieces of dynamite into his belt, and took two more in each hand. We peeked out before we left: the ruckus on the beach seemed to be even bigger. The watchman in the tower was asleep with his head resting on his crossed arms.

"What do we do now?"

"I'm going to explain it to you quickly. This is a circle, so you already know I'm going to do the four cardinal points. You do the others, even if you don't know their names."

"Okay."

"Over there where there are those round holes for planting trees later, that's where we put the dynamite. Dig, bury it, but leave the wick exposed."

"Are we going to light the wicks now?"

"Now, with a pile of soldiers and police on the beach? Of course not; but be ready."

"When you're finished we'll meet on Dona Libânia's sidewalk."

"Okay."

"And nobody tells on anybody if we're caught."

"Agreed. Courage, Comrade!"

We took off running, each of us heading in the direction of the cardinal points of his mission. I rounded a corner, found the first hole. The sand was soft. I dug and saw that I had lingered too long because I was burying the two sticks of dynamite standing up, and that was a waste of time. At the second hole I had already decided to bury the bars lying down, like two people who lie close to each other in the cemetery, but here the sand was harder and digging bruised my fingers.

When I was on my way to the fourth hole—I think it was the point between south and west, maybe you could call it south of the west—in my sweaty-fingered rushing around the dynamite fell out of my hand and went rolling off on its own like a cat running away in fear. I heard voices at the gate. I hid, trying to see where the dynamite had stopped rolling. I heard footsteps on the other side of the wall and I started to shudder with fear. I was going to get caught and they were going to find the dynamite, too.

"Unexpected problems, Comrade?"

3.14's voice had never hit me so clearly. He laughed as he looked at me, because he could see that I was terrified. He handed me the missing stick of dynamite.

"Are yours already done, Pi?"

"Yeah. The sand was really hard but I had the wire cutters to dig with. Let's go place your last one."

"Yeah, let's go. There's nobody here?"

"I don't think so. All quiet. But we have to step on it, we still have to finish the most complicated part of the plan."

"What's that?"

"I'll tell you in a minute. Hey, I buried mine lying down so I didn't waste time."

"Yeah, me too."

With the wire cutters acting as a spade it went a lot faster, but the sand at the final point was still soft. 3.14 looked up from where we were standing, pressed right up against the central part of the Mausoleum. That peaked mountain of cement looked just like a rocket that was ready for lift-off.

"It's a lot of cement." 3.14 looked worried.

"Should we set more dynamite?"

"We don't have time."

He moved closer to the wall and looked inside through a window without a pane, which opened on pure darkness. Then he looked at his feet.

"This is what I was looking for. I knew I'd seen this trench."

"What trench?"

Right around the Mausoleum was a kind of small groove, cut into the cement, as though it were a path made so that the ants wouldn't have any doubts about where to go, or invent new paths with twists and turns, as they liked to do. It was a flaw in the cement, a sort of narrow mini passageway that had been laid out in an enormous circle that linked up those holes where we had placed the dynamite.

"You see? A great idea of those Soviets—they don't even know how they're helping us. It must be for irrigation, to allow the water to circulate."

"So?"

"So the problem of our fuse is solved."

"But we don't have any wire to light dynamite to join up the cardinal points."

"We don't need wire. We just need 'hod drink,' as Gudafterov says."

"I get it!"

"That's all we're lacking, Comrade. Then we make a fuse with the drink linking up with the hiding-place of our choice. And then we light it."

"They do it with gasoline in the movies."

"But 'hod drink' will do it, too. I saw a house get set on fire in a movie with half a bottle of whisky."

"There aren't any leftovers in granma's house. Every last drop was drunk at the farewell party."

"But I know of someone who can help us."

"Who?"

"Comrade Charlita. It's time for a change of venue."

We ran again, slipping out through the hole in the fence, turned into the alley and only stopped when we reached Dona Libânia's sidewalk.

"Are you playing, children?" Sometimes Dona Libânia was like Granma Catarina: she appeared without making noise.

"Yes, Dona Libânia."

"Then you've already been to see what's happening out there on the beach?" She was looking for information.

"We've just come from there. The Soviets are trying to forbid everybody from entering the beach. They say they have orders from some general to close the beach because of I don't know what-all about the expansion of the construction site."

"You heard that over there on the beach?"

"Yes, just now."

"But the sand you have on your feet doesn't come from the beach."

"Goodbye, Dona Libânia. We've got to get going."

We moved along a short distance and took the opportunity to sit down on Senhor Tuarles's sidewalk to see if it was possible to speak to Charlita.

Dona Isabel sat on the veranda of their house, holding the AK-47 in her lap as though it were a baby. This happened a lot, I don't know why; Senhor Tuarles never went looking for his AK-47, not even when he was in a rush. One night we were woken up by loud noises in the chicken coop. It seems that Granma Catarina had seen figures moving around in the yard and had phoned Senhor Tuarles to warn him and see if he could come and take a look at what was going on. Granma Nineteen saw everything from the window of her room: Senhor Tuarles came out in his boxer shorts as far as the wall of his house—I figure it must have been about two in the morning—and peered into Granma Nineteen's yard. Then he whirled around and said in a loud voice that was heard by all: "Isabel, go upstairs and get the AK-47."

When he went to beat the shit out of the priest, I think the same thing happened: he went on foot as far as the church, he was nervous the whole way there, warning everybody that he was going to kill the priest because he had "done it" with the little girls of Bishop's Beach. Dona Isabel walked behind him, pleading with him to calm down, but only once they were close to the Kinanga Cinema did he remember to say: "Isabel, go get the AK-47."

I figure that memories are invisible restless tinglings that stay inside people. When I remember that stuff I start to laugh to myself until 3.14 asks me if I'm crazy to laugh alone like that.

"I'm just remembering stuff."

"But you're not an elder yet; you can't have much to remember."

"They've already told me lots of things about the old days. I'm laughing at old things, Pi."

"Old things aren't very funny."

"It depends, Pi. It depends."

There was Dona Isabel with the AK-47 in her lap waiting, because at any moment Senhor Tuarles might make a sign for her to bring it to him. These were the things that 3.14 didn't understand, but that made me laugh: after handing over the AK-47 to Senhor Tuarles, what Dona Isabel had to do, which was what Senhor Tuarles wanted Dona Isabel to do, was to stand there for a long time begging him not to use the AK-47, nor to threaten anyone, nor even to put a bullet in the magazine. And

Senhor Tuarles always did the same thing, uttering the same sentence: "It's all right, Isabel. You can put the AK-47 away."

As Senhor Tuarles remained far away, getting worked up by the arguments and not making any sign, Dona Isabel went upstairs to put away the AK-47. We heard a feeble whistle coming from the old chicken coop. Charlita was calling us.

"Charlita, we've come to talk to you."

"If my dad catches you..."

"It's a last favour. The mission's moving forward."

"I don't want to know about it."

"Please, you don't need to talk to us anymore. Just get a bottle of hot drink and leave it here on the wall. We'll grab it from Granma Nineteen's house."

"Hot drink?"

"Yes, some drink like whisky or whatever."

"How am I gonna know?"

"Open it and smell it. The strongest one is the one you want."

"It can't be rubbing alcohol?"

"I don't think so because it'll disappear before we set it alight."

"What are you guys gonna set alight?"

"You said you didn't want to know about it."

"All right." Her face grew pensive. "After nine o'clock I'll leave it on the wall."

"Okay. Affirmative."

We heard voices singing really out-of-tune songs in Soviet which, even without understanding the lyrics, gave you a headache just to listen to them. We went to Granma Nineteen's veranda, climbed up onto the wall and saw the drunken soldiers singing and drinking even more.

"That's a really good sign. Let them keep on drinking."

"I'm thinkin' about something, 3.14."

"Don't start with your tales."

"It's not that. But we can't blow everything up with people inside."

"Listen, Comrade, it sounds like you ain't understanding this business clearly. Today they're going to close the beach, tomorrow they may start telling people to pack their bags, and the day after tomorrow, thanks to that dynamite you saw today, you may be imprisoned in that bathroom of your gran-ma's where you all hide from the lightning during thunder-storms." 3.14 was speaking in a low voice, very close to my face. "Today those tupariovs are all drunk and nobody's going to sleep at the construction site, and if somebody does spend the night there, well, too bad."

"What do you mean, too bad? Are you crazy? If somebody dies we're going straight to a war zone in a plane that'll take us away in the middle of the night without waiting for morning."

"Jeeze, will you stop that! Nobody knows anything and nobody sleeps at the construction site."

"And what if the body of the Comrade President is there?"

"You really think so? They're only going to bring the body on the day of the inauguration. They're not gonna leave an embalmed corpse to sleep in that darkness with all the dust from the construction."

"And all the birds?"

"The birds—too bad! They may just take off."

"How? Poor little things."

"Maybe the cages'll burst open and they'll be able to fly away."

"It's not worth it, 3.14. You know very well that's not gonna happen. They're locked into those tight little cages and they're gonna die, either in the explosion or from inhaling the fumes of the fire."

"You're not gettin' it, Comrade. This mission's no joke. If it doesn't happen today, when they're all hammered, they'll find the dynamite that we buried. They're gonna see that the boxes are open, and they're gonna put watchmen on the site. It has to be today!"

"And if Charlita doesn't get the 'hod drink'?"

"We're gonna have to light the fuses."

"There isn't enough time."

"Yes, there is. I looked at the wicks: they're short. We'll just light four of them. I take north and west, you take south and east."

"There isn't enough time, 3.14." I felt really sad and frightened. "We'll die from being dexploded. They won't even be able to find our bodies to bury us."

"Shut your trap. Listen carefully: there's enough time, we just don't run away in the direction of the houses. That's what there's not time for."

"So?"

"We light the fuses and we run and dive into the sea. It's the closest exit, and we stay under the foam so that the flames don't get us."

"Sure. Maybe Charlita will get the booze."

"Let's hope so."

Events just kept happening. For me, it was too many things all in the same day.

A very polished jeep arrived at very high speed at the edge of the beach, circled around the square, then braked suddenly. Soldiers jumped out with AK-47s in their hands and did what in the movies is called "covering their positions." It looked like a war zone.

The Russian soldiers, even in the midst of the chaos, stopped their arguments and they all stood at attention in a line. They looked like they were in the schoolyard and would start singing the national anthem at any moment. I laughed again.

"What you laughin' about now?"

"I'm thinking what it would be like if somebody ordered those soldiers to sing our national anthem...Just imagine the accent and the lyrics they'd use!"

"Sure, it'd be pretty funny."

Judging by the difference in his uniform and his walk, this must be the Boss General that Gudafterov was always talking about. The Soviet workers, including Dimitry and Gudafterov, saluted and took up positions at the back of the formation. As for the Angolans, they didn't move.

"Go take a look, boys," Dona Libânia shouted. "Otherwise, how are we going to know what's going on?"

We set off running, trying to get close, but the soldiers with their AK-47s gave us terrifying looks. Sea Foam backed off too, and stood next to us and to the Comrade Gas Jockey.

"The highest rank of *el poder* has arrived." Sea Foam saluted with his left hand to tease them.

The Boss General spoke in Russian in short, harshly expelled words that only the soldiers understood. Next he called on Comrade Gudafterov, who came forward with a tombstone face that was painful to see.

Foam was getting closer and closer to us, trying not to make a sound.

"Son, hand in this missive to that granma of yours who has fewer digits than other granmas."

I thought he was joking or spouting nonsense, but he actually had a letter in his hand, and he was pointing it at me.

"Who, me?"

"The granma is yours and the letter is hers. Here, *compañero*, we do not make *errores*."

Furtively, he handed me the letter, as though it were a secret.

"Are you writing letters to my granma, Foam?"

We were all staring straight ahead, as though we, too, were in formation, and we spoke in very low voices out of fear of being caught by the soldiers with AK-47s.

"I don't write any more. ¡*Yo hablo*!" he said in a loud voice. "The letter is from a certain Bilhardov, also known on Bishop's Beach and the surrounding areas, as Comrade Armpitov. I have spoken!"

The very sweaty soldiers in the formation moved back a short distance, at an almost marching step, and let the Boss General pass. He went to speak with the Old Fisherman. We almost couldn't hear them.

"Comrades, beach close for temporary, orders of Comrade President: Workers must finish Muzzleum verk. Your collaboration, please."

"Lots of people work here every day, Comrade General. We need to go out on the sea. Some people still live on the other side of the beach."

"Comrade President resolve all problem. Today beach close. Reasons of security. Muzzleum almost finish. Need make verk beach zone. Nobody hurt. Comrade President promise. Population must collaborate. Last varning: tomorrow nobody on beach, soldiers close everything fast! Gudafter-noon, Comrades!"

He didn't go on trying to speak. Gudafterov went to open the main gate and the jeep entered the Mausoleum construction site. The soldiers in the jeep stayed at the gate to guard the entrance, and they ordered everyone to go away without putting up any more resistance.

"Time to come home, children," Granma Nineteen said from the veranda. "It's lunchtime and I don't want you over there around those guns."

Everybody cleared out. Senhor Tuarles, drenched in sweat, came over to say that the best thing would be for them to drink a few beers to freshen up and think up better ideas. Sea Foam ran into his house, the Comrade Gas Jockey leaned back his chair and set his hat at an angle that allowed his eyes to grow sleepy.

"After lunch you come here and tell the whole conversation," Dona Libânia said. "You can eat slices of a banana cake that was left over from the party, but don't tell anybody."

"Sure, Dona Libânia." 3.14 had a sweet tooth.

"Listen, Pi, do you think they're gonna find the dynamite we put there?"

"No way. He's just going there to bawl people out. He's gonna find the soldiers drunk, he's gonna give a couple of them a smack to make an example of them. You think the General's not hungry? He must want to have lunch, too."

"Let's hope."

"Hey, when you finish eating let's meet out front here again. There could be more surprises."

"I hope not."

"Don't forget to give the letter to your granma. Then you can tell me what's in it. Imagine the mistakes in Armpitov's writing!"

"Sure thing."

I went to the bathroom to wash my hands, take off my shirt and wash my armpits, and wash my face with that soap that came with little crumbs trapped inside it, I don't know why. It was very hot and the letter fell out of my waist where I had it hidden. I opened the letter. It was two pages long, written in a handwriting that was difficult to read. It seemed to have been written in haste; it was impossible to understand anything. But it was from him: it even had his signature—Bilhardov—at the end.

I stood still for a moment thinking. Words, the words that one person sometimes says to another person, at times they're words that a person speaks without thinking, especially when they're arguing, they just come out like that; at other times they're words that a person spends a long time preparing, because they mean something to the other person, and can be said only with well-prepared words, and it's not even always good to prepare words too much; at times talking at random or really fast summons up words that have more truth or force of conviction. That two-page letter, with words written in haste, yet thought out with a view to being read by my Granma Nineteen—what words would those be? Why had Gudafterov written such a long letter to my granma? Maybe he was coming by again with his conversation about the beauty of "snov," and the forests and hearths of his cold country in the far-away; maybe he had even succeeded in writing a beautiful letter and—I had already seen this in the movies—women of any age like beautiful letters that make them cry.

I crumpled the letter, tore it into little pieces and dropped it in the toilet to flush away Comrade Gudafterov's words.

"Go write letters to your own darn wife there in the far-away." I grabbed the water bucket and poured the whole thing into the toilet so that no paper remained.

"What's the hold-up? Come to the table," Granma called.

"Sorry, Granma, I was washing my face. It's really hot."

"Come and sit down. And I don't want to see any elbows on the table."

During lunch I saw the Boss General's jeep pass by the window really fast, with the soldiers aiming their AK-47s at the sky. It made me nervous, and I wondered if they'd found the dynamite buried at the cardinal points 3.14 invented. Some day I'm going to ask André the commando if they also have that code of cardinal points in war zones, because I figured it was an awesome idea of Pi's—unless he had seen it in a movie and not told me about it.

"Granma, can I go play?"

"Right after eating, with this sun on your head? Perish the thought. We're going to take a siesta."

It was better not to argue. Insisting too much might put Granma in a bad mood, and then she might send me to lie down for the whole afternoon. I needed not to get angry at her in order to be free later in the afternoon, or even at night, whatever turned out to be the time to grab the "hod drink."

"Can I go to Granma Catarina's room?"

"No. You're going to lie down in my bed."

"All right, Granma."

"If you fall asleep, I'll wake you later. Today Doctor Rafael is coming here. You can help me understand what he says."

"Late in the afternoon, Granma?"

"I think so, I'm not sure."

"But I've already agreed to go play with 3.14 then."

"You can play later. I'll let you go out afterwards."

Granma must have been tired, or sleepy from the pills she was taking for the pain: she soon fell asleep next to me. I heard a few whistles from downstairs but I was unable to open the window, because it might have woken Granma up.

I rolled over very gently and entered Granma Catarina's room. She was rocking in her chair.

"Granma, just let me open the window a moment."

"Open it, son. It's all the same to me."

Down below, 3.14, drenched in sweat by the midday sun—I don't even want to imagine the smell of his b.o.-dorov—was calling out to me to come downstairs. In his hand he had a letter identical to the one I had drowned in the bathroom. Annoyed, I went downstairs.

"Where are you going? Aren't you supposed to be sleeping? I'm going to tell on you," Madalena said, and started up the stairs.

"Listen carefully, Madalena: if you tell Granma that I went out, I swear I'm going to tell her about all the times I saw you smooching with a Soviet soldier, and also with another Angolan soldier, and I'm also going to tell about the time on Saturday night when I saw you come in at close to two in the morning, when even the clock in the living room was striking the hour, and you were wearing that miniskirt that Granma already forbid you to wear because it's so short, and I'm going to tell her about the baths you take in the white foam of the sea with that boy, even when the water is cold or full of jellyfish. Do you hear me?"

Madalena's face was so fearful that it looked as if she was going to faint. She stood still, looking at me, and only later said: "I'm sorry. You can go. I was just joking."

3.14 was waiting for me, half-concealed, amidst the trees.

"Listen to this: it looks like Gudafterov mined the beach with letters for your granma." He laughed.

"I don't find that funny at all."

"What did the other letter say?"

"I don't know. It was unreadable. I threw it away."

"It was your Aunt Adelaide who gave me this one. She said that Gudafterov left it with her to hand in to your granma."

"Son of a bitch."

"If you want, I can try to read it."

"Open it quickly. I escaped from bed. My granma's sleeping."

We tore open the envelope and the letter resembled the other one, but the handwriting was more difficult and it was impossible to understand anything. It started with *Deer Komrad Frend Dona Nhéte*, and after that you could hardly make out anything.

"Look at this. He wrote the word 'explosion.'"

"Are you sure?"

"Don't you see it then? It's written 'explozhun,' which must be 'explosion' in Russian."

"But my granma doesn't understand Russian."

"You aín't gettin' it; it must be a tattletale letter. He must be telling on us about the dynamite."

"Son of a bitch."

"If you want, we'll burn the letter right now. I brought matches."

"Sure. You burn it. I'm going back to the room."

"What? And are you coming back?"

"I can only do it late in the afternoon. We're waiting for Rafael KnockKnock's visit."

"Okay."

Granma Nineteen was sleeping when I returned to the room, and it must have been a deep sleep because she was snoring rather loudly.

I didn't find Granma Catarina in the room, nor was she in the bathroom, and Madalena Kamussekele hadn't seen her either. An almost oppressive sadness swamped my chest, and that's not just blather; it was right in the chest that I got a strange feeling. I went to bed but was unable to fall asleep.

I got up again and went to Granma Catarina's room. Everything was tidied up, the black shawl folded on the bed next to the pillow, on the bedside table were photos of all of the grandchildren and a thread, black also, was attached to a freshly polished silver crucifix. The mirror, too, was cleaner than on other days, and the window was closed and locked. There was no smell of any sort to indicate that someone had been there a short time before. It seemed like a lie, or a disappearance in the movies.

"Granma Catarina?" The words issued from my lips very gently, but there was no reply.

Never again was there a reply. Never again did Granma Catarina appear. She didn't say goodbye to me, nor did she warn me that she couldn't speak with me any longer, not even in secret without my telling anyone. It must be because Granma Catarina really didn't like farewells. She always used to say: "You see, in the old days people were people who arrived. We didn't know how to take our farewell."

I sat down on the bed. I don't like farewells at all, either, Granma Catarina, I thought, and in the big mirror, I saw myself seated there. I started to dredge up memories of moments or conversations with Granma Catarina in order to see whether at some point she would come into the room—but there was nothing.

"Do you know things about the future, Granma Catarina?" I asked her one day when she sat down next to me at the breakfast table.

"The future is full of difficult things that happen in a different way each time. I prefer to divine the past."

She didn't like to speak to a lot of people in those last years and not even Granma Nineteen liked it very much when the children said they had been with Granma Catarina at either breakfast time, or at any other.

"But why? Granma Catarina always talks with us. Why can't we tell anyone about it? Why?"

"Because you can't."

It was a response children heard often. "You can't go play because"; or, if it was a little later, and darker out, "because I say so." Going to the beach when the sea was rough, skipping class when you didn't feel like going to school in the morning, didn't want to get a vaccination, didn't want to go to the dentist, playing in the dusty square when the water truck was damping down the earth, standing beneath the rain with mouth and arms open when it rained hard, wearing red blouses if it was thundering, having fun with crazy Sea Foam, asking Dona Libânia why she wasn't married, asking Senhor Tuarles why his other daughters didn't wear glasses so that they could see the soap operas properly, eating green mangoes with salt, staying in bed until noon, it was all not allowed "because you can't." But there must be a reason for these things and the elders could at least do us the favour of telling us instead of keeping this secret to themselves.

"Hey, *¿hay alguien aquí?*"

I heard the voice of the Comrade Doctor Rafael Knock-Knock come up the stairs to find me seated in Granma Catarina's dark, empty room, without Granma Catarina there to talk to me. To tell the truth, it's not your voice that I wanted to hear, I thought, and I went downstairs.

"*¿Cómo estás, compañero*? I'm here to see your *abuela*. How is she?"

"She's sleeping like a log."

"Like a log?"

"That's when a person is sleeping so that it's really hard to wake them up."

"Can you call your *abuela*?"

"It's still early, Doctor. She likes to sleep for a bit at this time and I can't disturb the dreams she must be dreaming."

"Really?"

"Yes. Could you wait a moment?"

"Yes. Why not?"

We went out onto the veranda. At that hour there was already a shadow close to the wall.

"Look, you know all this is going to *desaparecer*, no?"

"The Mausoleum? Yeah, it looks like it's going."

"No, no. Bishop's Beach—the houses, *todo*. I've seen *los planes*. The fallout will be very beautiful."

"Falling out, falling over..."

"*¿Cómo?*"

"Of course, *compañero*... Of course."

"What are you saying?"

"I wanted to ask you one more question."

"Go ahead."

"Can somebody do something a little bit bad so that they can do something good later?"

"*Bueno*... I think so, *sí*."

"And if the person were a child, could they still do it?"

"Listen, *compañero*." Doctor Rafael laid his hand on my shoulder. I thought he was going to start making his "Knock-Knock" jokes, but that wasn't it. "There are things that one has to do that others will never understand. This happens. They are *secretos* that only your heart can understand."

"'*Secretos*' are secrets?"

"Yes."

"I like the word 'secrets.' It's like something mysterious that lots of things fit inside."

"*Me gusta* your way of thinking. Maybe you will become a *poeta*."

"I don't want to, thanks. I heard that poets end up going crazy."

"No, it's not true. *Los poetas* are mad, but it is another type of madness. Do not worry...Do you think it is time to wake up your *abuela*?"

"Yes, I'm going to call her. Sorry, I even forgot to ask if you want something to drink, comrade?"

"*Sí*. What do you have?"

"A good glass of water, not chilled because we don't have electricity."

"That would be good, *gracias*."

While Madalena brought him the tepid water, I went to wake up Granma Nineteen.

"Granma, Comrade KnockKnock is here."

"He's here already? I have to brush my hair. Tell him I'll be down in a minute."

While Granma was distracted in the living room, with the doctor examining her lesion, I went outside to see if anything was happening in the square.

The Comrade Gas Jockey, Foam and Comrade Dimitry were arguing with each other with worried faces around the gas pump.

"You don't even know the rumours that are being spread." 3.14 came out of the bushes.

"You frightened me."

"Comrade Gudafterov has disappeared. Everybody's at the construction site lookin' for him. I mean, Comrade Dimitry's lookin' for him. The soldiers are all drunk and some of them have already gone home."

"How did he disappear?"

"I don't know, maybe he drowned."

"Drowned? What kind of tale's that?"

"I don't think the blue lobsters know how to swim. How is it that they stand here every day sweating in that uniform, right next to the sea, looking at the bright blue water, and they never feel like jumping in? It must be that they don't know how to swim."

"It can't be that. You may not know how to swim, but you can still jump into the foam, like Foam does."

"But they'd be ashamed that we'd give them a hard time for the rest of their lives."

"No...I figure this tale about Gudafterov has to do with the letters."

"Hey, you must be right."

"We're gonna try to read it again."

"Read it again? Only if you can read ashes. I burnt the letter."

"It's better if we don't say anything to anybody. There might have been something important in the letter."

The afternoon didn't want to end. No sooner did the sun approach the sea so that blackness could come and we could carry out our mission, than I began to feel nervous about it, and about the strange things that were happening on Bishop's Beach. Granma Catarina wasn't there any more, Gudafterov had disappeared, and Doctor Rafael had confirmed all of the plans about making the houses of our Bishop's Beach disappear.

"The afternoon doesn't want to end, 3.14. Everything's so slow."

"Get a grip and calm down. The Mausoleum's quiet, Gudafterov has disappeared, there's just the man in the watchtower left, and he won't leave there even to go pee-pee."

"He's the one who could see us."

"Only if they turn on the big surge light. They didn't turn it on last night. It could be burned out."

"But do you say 'surge light' or 'searchlight'?"

"You say, 'That big light that lights up the area we want to get through without getting caught,' you smart-ass!"

"Calm down. It was just a doubt I had about the Portuguese language."

"You know, you've got a lot of doubts. I've been thinkin'—but I'm not going to give the idea to Comrade Dimitry."

"What idea?"

"To find Gudafterov,"—3.14 started to laugh—"all they've got to do is follow the aroma of the b.o.-dorov! Ha ha!"

Time didn't want to pass. It reminded me of that poem we read in school about the lazy train that didn't want to keep rolling forward along the railway line because it knew that the line had been diverted and that at the end of the day it wasn't going to reach a station; it was going to be taken, by the same engineer who had worked on it for years, to a huge garage where it would be dismantled.

"You remember that poem?"

"I don't remember anything, and I'm guessing you're makin' stuff up."

"I swear I'm not making stuff up. That tale even ended with the engineer abandoning the train on the track and being fired because he didn't have the courage to take the train to the garage where they dismantled trains that couldn't run anymore."

"So was it a poem or a tale?"

"That's not important. Now you're the one who has too many doubts. What's important, and what I don't remember, is whether or not the train was dismantled."

"My dad was fired, too." 3.14's voice was all sad.

"Seriously?"

"Yes. They fired almost all the workers at the Mausoleum construction site."

When the sun approached the horizon, the wind that usually arrived with it did not come.

On the veranda, Granma Nineteen smiled as she chatted with Doctor Rafael KnockKnock, and from where we stood we could see Dona Libânia pressed against the wall of the veranda to hear the conversation better.

Sea Foam came running out of his house, passed by the other side of the garbage dump, his legs leaping along the shoreline like he himself were running as though he wished to fly, balancing with his bare feet on the white sea foam of Bishop's Beach.

"What's he got hanging from his body?"

"Aren't those his dreadlocks?"

"That long? They look like ropes."

The sun sank, yellowed, into the dark blue of the sea and invented a beautiful sunset of a mulatto colour no words could capture. We just stared.

Time had decided it could pass.

And I stood still.

It wasn't only the fingers or the toes, the legs or the head and eyes, that liked to look one way then the other. It was stillness itself. Within me. The voice that speaks within me had nothing to say, or else it wanted to practise a silence just like that.

Still from not thinking.

To feel the evening? To await a signal from the wind, a whistle like a segregated conversation taking account of the fact that the birds cried in a far-away and I could hear them? Wanting to hear mysterious sentences from Granma Catarina? Contemplating the things of Bishop's Beach that I thought I alone saw?

Inventing minutes that were mine within the minutes of time?

Growing up with a heart and body that were fleeing from childhood? "Is someone running behind the child?" Granma Nineteen was in the habit of asking. Was time pursuing me with a body to frighten me? I felt the whole world there in the small square of Bishop's Beach.

Nor did 3.14 say anything.

The two of us were still, imitating the ants when they stop for a tiny second to rest from their work, or the grasshopper stirring its body to get ready for a jump. Or the slug, still, lying on top of its spittle as though it could speak with the moon. Or sleeping fish.

"Don't fish sleep even a little bit, Pi?"

"You should ask that crazy question of yours to the Old Fisherman. Did you ever see fish standing still with their eyes closed, almost throbbing with sleepiness?"

"I've heard it said that fish are really forgetful. It must be good to be like that."

"Not remembering places and things? Forget it."

"Aren't there some things you'd like to forget?"

"I don't think so. I like my life full of things that I can still tell to someone. If I have seven children, how am I going to have enough good tales to tell?"

"You want to have seven children?"

"I do."

"Don't worry about the tales. The tales that make the best stories are the ones we invent."

"You think so?"

"I think so."

Not even an eddy of dust to divert the eyes. It seemed like nothing wanted to happen.

"Are we just gonna stand here?"

"Yeah."

"Doing what?"

"Just sitting. 'Watching the time go by,' as the elders say."

"It's really dark on Bishop's Beach. I don't know if time's going to want to pass by here."

3.14 drew an arrow in the sand, pointing in the direction of Granma Nineteen's house. Then a heart and two well-drawn figurines.

"If Gudafterov is slow off the mark with your granma, I figure the Socialist Republic of Cuba is going to make some forward strides."

I looked at the veranda. The two of them looked very calm as they conversed, and I really enjoyed seeing Granma Nineteen with that smile that I could only guess at because I was unable to see their faces.

"I don't like that conversation."

"But Gudafterov already invited your granma to go with him there to the far-away, right?"

"What do I know? It could just be some tale of my granma's."

"But if the *muchacho* doctor invites her, well excuse me, but Cuba is a lot better."

"What do you know?"

"I don't know anything, but Cuba's got sun, beaches and pretty mulattas, I saw it all on television. Do you want to compare that with snow, frozen water that turns into ice and whitish women with minuscule boobs?"

"Yeah, you're right."

I thought I heard something in the yard.

"Did you hear something?"

"Nothing. What?"

"Hold it."

Something, yes, close to the wall that divided Senhor Tuarles's house from Granma Nineteen's house.

"The parrots?"

"What kind of parrot's that? It's Charlita."

We ran forward, then went in stealthily along the side of the veranda so that Granma wouldn't call us. The yard was dark. The parrot His Name shouted out to expose us: "Down with American imperialism." We made an effort not to laugh: the words came from a television commercial that hadn't run in a long time. Just Parrot finished off: "Hey, Reagan, hands off Angola."

We passed beneath the fig tree. Where the wall was lowest, we met up with Charlita.

"How come you guys don't pay any attention? I've been here, like, forever, and those parrots did everything but call out my name."

"You're ahead of schedule, Comrade."

"My dad fell asleep in the living room watching the news in African languages. It's now or never. Here's the stuff."

"Wonderful Comrade Charlita!"

She passed over a nearly full bottle of whisky with a really piercing aroma that looked good for the mission.

"You figure it'll do?"

"It should," 3.14 said, sniffing it and closing it again. "I'm going to recommend to Comrade Gudafterov that you be decorated."

"I'm going to be what?" In addition to her poor sight, I'm not sure if Charlita heard very well.

"Decorated. You may receive a medal to show the gratitude of the community of Bishop's Beach." He laughed.

"But is it gratitude, or is it a gratuity?"

"Stop that, we've got to get out of here."

Charlita's voice trembled. "Good luck," she said, almost as though we were heading for the war zone at any moment.

"Thank you, Comrade. Long live the revolution!"

"Tupariov," she joked.

Charlita disappeared and then tripped on something that couldn't be anything important because the old chicken coop was completely empty.

"You okay?"

"Yeah. Just go."

We ran away, passing close to the water tank. The parrots continued to be restless. I dipped my hand in a pool of leftover dirty, soapy water.

"What are you doing?"

"It's to make the parrots calm down."

I sprinkled their cage twice with the water. It was what Madalena did; they put their troubles behind them with drops of that leftover blue-soap water. They licked their bodies and remained still, saying nothing.

"Those parrots have a screw loose." 3.14 didn't know about this method of silencing parrots.

"Let's just get going."

"And your granma on the veranda?"

"Before we get to the veranda, we'll jump over into Senhor Tuarles's yard. We'll go out the other side."

"What if she calls you?"

"Too bad. We've got the bottle now, we have to get going."

"What about dinner? My dad's gonna give me a thrashing."

"Too bad," I laughed. "That's your problem. Charlita moved the mission forward, now there's no dinner for anybody. Draw courage from your hunger."

"Okay. We'll move ahead. Liquid ready?"

"Affirmative."

"Matches?"

"I don't know. Do you have them?"

"I have them. Dynamite in position?"

"Affirmative."

"Forward, Comrade."

We leapt, deliberately so as not to make noise, and in the right places. In spite of the darkness, we knew all the pitfalls of the houses on Bishop's Beach, and with the two of us together it was practically impossible to put a foot wrong. "Careful with those bricks next to Senhor Tuarles's abandoned car," I warned, and we circumvented them. "Lift the gate or it's going to make noise." We got out without anyone seeing us.

"Should we crawl until we get to the entrance to the alley, going past your granma's sidewalk, or are we going to be intercepted?"

"It's better not to. The problem is that Dona Libânia has secret techniques for seeing and hearing, and at this time of night she could tell on us for skipping dinner or something."

"Affirmative. We'll circle around."

The circle was enormous and we had to try to hide the bottle because this in itself was suspicious; anyone who saw us running flat-out through the darkness with that whisky bottle would tell on us.

"Where are you going?"

We stopped short in fear, almost ceasing to breathe.

"Foam! Do you always have to show up like a ghost from the other world?" 3.14 even forgot that he was crazy.

"*La vida es como es.* Where are you going?"

"We're just gonna deliver something."

"Something? A secret?"

"Foam, keep your voice down. We'll tell you later."

"Later, later...When later? In ten years? Twenty-five years? Time is always passing...Are you going to the Mausoleum?" How could he know this? "Lots of people want to go to the Mausoleum at this time of night...*Yo lo sé* because...The birds... The colourful flock...You guys are mixed up in that, eh?" He spoke in a louder voice.

"Shhh, Foam. Just go your own way."

"My way is the way of us all."

"Keep your voice down. We're on a mission here."

"And I am on a *misión* here, too." And he didn't ask anything more.

We waited a moment. Concealing the bottle, 3.14 looked at me.

"We will do the following, *compañeros*...You go on that side and I'll go past Dona Liberia's place,"—he sometimes called Dona Libânia this—"and we'll see who gets there first."

I was about to say something, but Pi didn't let me.

"Agreed. Now let's go."

Foam ran off happily. He disappeared into the darkness, bidding us goodbye and tripped away with his long dreadlocks.

"Isn't it dangerous for him?"

"No. They'll stop him at the entrance. Or even on the beach—there must be watchmen there."

"I don't know."

"I don't know either, and I don't want to know. Everybody has to deal with his own problems."

We ran with caution through the darkness. Aside from potholes in the sidewalks, open sewers and damaged transformer boxes near which it was dangerous to pee, Bishop's Beach had many trees with spreading roots in places where a person wouldn't expect them.

We passed Paulinho's house and the big house of Carmen Fernández's father, and cut through the alley of André the commando's house.

"Whoa, kids, you runnin' around at this time of night? What happens if the cops pick you up?"

"André, how's it goin'?" I stepped forward so that Pi could hide the bottle.

"Great, and you guys?"

"Yeah, the usual."

"And the parrot His Name, he still alive?"

"He's really good and he eats a ton."

"Those parrots that were in the war are always starving. Where are you guys goin'?"

"Just out for a walk."

"A walk in the dark?"

"We're fed up with walkin' in the afternoon with the sun on our heads. Now we're tryin' out takin' a spin in the dark, like a reconnaissance mission, you get it?"

"I get it." He pretended to believe us. "And you're goin' along this side of the construction site? Won't the Soviets give you a hard time?"

"Today all the Soviets are drunk. They got told off for it."

"Go ahead then. If you have any problems just say you're André the commando's cousin."

"That's cool."

We started running again, and our heartbeats accelerated when we found ourselves already on the other side, close to the wire mesh fence, in near-total darkness, with only a filament from the waning moon to give us limited visibility.

The light was off in the more distant watchtower. We could only see the one that was closer badly, with the watchman seated there, unmoving.

"It's really silent and the lights are off in the towers."

"Their generator's broken, or else they forgot to fuel it."

"Let's go."

"But what's the plan?"

"Again?"

"Whaddya mean, again? Are you thick? We've got to damp down the whole path between the sticks of dynamite, that I know. But there's only one bottle. How are we going to do it?"

"Ah, you're right. We'll have to activate our back-up plan," 3.14 said.

"Jargon, again. Speak in clear Portuguese."

"I'm going to douse the whole left side while you cover me by watching to see if anyone comes. If someone appears, Angolan, Soviet or even Cuban, we only came here to play. You whistle to warn me, I hide the bottle and we split."

"Okay. Now, go."

"Wait a sec. I just thought of something." 3.14 was checking the materials, setting down the bottle and the matches.

"What is it now?"

"It's better if you go first. The left side is really dark. You see better in the dark."

"You come up with the craziest stuff."

"Just go. I'll wait for you here."

I set off at a run like a hunched-over commando.

I found the first cardinal point, but something was odd. The ground was almost invisible, but the thread of the fuse and the dynamite were there. There was a kind of white sand in the hole and in the small groove that connected it to the next stick of dynamite. I sniffed.

I couldn't waste time. I doused the hole and started to spill whisky along the tiny groove in the earth. I looked behind me and saw that the damp stain dried up quickly. I wasn't certain that the whisky would even link up the cardinal points with a well-lighted fire.

At the second cardinal point the dynamite wasn't even visible. I dug down a little and felt the coolness on my hands. I tested with my finger and it was what I had thought: someone had poured coarse salt in our dynamite holes.

I didn't have time to think. I soaked the second point and half of the groove that connected to the third hole. I saw a very thin thread of salt that led out of there and into the interior of the Mausoleum by way of a door that we had never seen.

The guard in the tower coughed and got up to stretch his arms. I quickly entered the tiny door to hide because it was possible that he, too, saw well in the darkness, or that he had those glasses from the movies that see in the night in a greenish colour.

Inside it was dark and damp. I closed my eyes hard to get myself used to the darkness, and I saw as far as my eyes could see: the interior of the Mausoleum seemed to be a really dark, web-like pattern made out of that coarse salt. I don't know how they had done it; maybe it was a Soviet construction technique. The salt was stuck together and climbed the walls like the threads of sand left by a termite when it climbed a tree. The patterns crossed each other and climbed farther than I could see. In some places there was much more salt that also crossed some cardboard boxes that looked like hastily wrapped presents. I felt afraid and I left: it looked like the web of a giant trap.

I "proceeded with the mission," as Comrade 3.14 would have said, and arrived at the third cardinal point with the path well doused with whisky. From there, looking through narrowed eyes, I could see the sea in a calm, windless darkness. The sea is always so big and beautiful at any hour of the day, becalmed or with waves that drive boats across it, green in the sunlight or burning blue in imitation of the blues in the sky in the daytime.

I had to cut short these thoughts, which could have delayed me even more. When I had puddled the whisky around the fourth cardinal point, which in reality was only half of the eight dynamite-primed holes, I was gripped by the fear of failing in my mission, almost to the point of tears: the whisky had run out.

I started running again, almost without hunching over, and found 3.14 lying on the ground, very calm, with a little matchstick in his mouth that looked like Lucky Luke's cigarette when he's about to draw his gun faster than his own shadow. I lay down alongside him so that we could pretend that we were in the combat trenches.

"I'm startin' to see that it's even better if you do the other four points. You're awesome at seein' in the dark."

"Lower your voice, Pi," I interrupted. "We don't have enough whisky and the watchman in the tower just woke up."

"The whisky's finished?" He became serious.

"The whisky was done in no time because those concrete grooves are enormous."

"How far did it last?"

"Up to the fourth point. We've still got to do all of the other side."

"Only if Charlita provisions us with more fuel."

"Provisions, provisions...This is a fine time for you to break out your military Portuguese. We don't have time."

"You're right." He paused in a strange way. "You ready?"

"For what?"

"It has to be now. If we retreat, the whisky evaporates. And we don't have another hour to come back here. They must already be looking for us for dinner."

"Now? How?"

"I also brought this little flask of alcohol. It's our fallback measure. We go as far as the alcohol lasts, then we ignite it."

"And we take off running..."

"You got it."

My hands trembled. 3.14's did, too, as he picked up the flask of alcohol as if sliding a bullet into the chamber of Senhor Tuarles's AK-47 and placing a dead-eye shot into a huge load of dynamite.

Far out on the beach a tiny light flickered and went out. Maybe it was the Old Fisherman lighting his pipe or starting a bonfire on the seashore. A thought, after all, is like that quick light and does not linger long.

"Let's get igniting, Comrade."

We doused the first cardinal point with alcohol and traced a line that passed under the metal fence as far as an enormous tree. There we lay down in the trench of the tree's roots.

"The watchman in the tower is standing up, Pi."

"I'm going to light it, then we run. By the time he sees the fire, we're outa here."

"Light it!"

The first match produced a flame that illuminated the area around us and I saw the beautiful patterns on the old skin of that tree. Before the flame could light the alcohol, the match went out. 3.14 lit the second match closer and touched it to the alcohol. But nothing caught.

"You see, it's counterfeit alcohol."

"That doesn't exist."

"It does too exist. They even counterfeit that Monte Rio wine."

"Just light it quickly before the alcohol evaporates."

The third match caught fast and strong. It wasn't necessary to say anything: we took off running. We let everything go and looked like Foam running flat-out, but we tried to follow up with our eyes on the racing twists and turns made by the fire. It burst out of the trench of roots, made a turn, passed beneath the wire mesh, made another turn close to the watchtower, hit a straightaway and accelerated. We accelerated as well and came flying into Dona Libânia's yard, driven by our fear of the explosion because, in the end, we didn't know how much dynamite we had put there. We hunched over, waiting for the noise—but the fire burned itself out just past the tower.

Our mouths open in disbelief, feeling like crying again, we saw the fire suddenly fizzle without exploding eight cardinal points and a bottle of Senhor Tuarles's whisky.

"Son of a whorovsky," 3.14 said, and I thought he was complaining to the fire. "Couldn't he have pissed somewhere else?"

The watchman, up above, was pissing a river on the groove of our fire, even a little bit in front of the point where the alcohol was about to meet the whisky. We saw his posture up there with his legs spread, pissing on our explosion plan.

"Soviet tupariov," I said, just to say something and not feel like crying.

We couldn't say a word.

The two of us watched the guard return to his post in the tower, sit down and cross his arms to sleep. He hadn't even seen the fire.

"What's that?" A woman's voice filled us with supernatural fear. "Look over there!"

It was Dona Libânia, bent over behind us to point in the opposite direction, at a cardinal point that was after south and before west.

A whitish smoke was pouring out of the storage shed, where we had seen the birds and the dynamite; an enormous light that was not an explosion ignited itself like a big searchlight that hugged the ground as if trying to light up birds that fly at night.

"I don't know that thing's name," I said, looking, "but I've seen it in the movies."

"It's that light you put on when you're lost or you want the helicopter to find you."

Another enormous light, but green this time, came on and started to slide along on its own, at high speed; we saw only the green stain casting shadows in the area around the storage shed as it headed towards the wire mesh fence on the side that faced the sea.

That was where the first concentrated noise of a chain explosion like one hundred grenades in a bag blowing up at the same time took place. The green light accelerated more quickly. Dona Libânia said in a very low voice: "Oh, my God." I figure she didn't even have time to say "God." Another powerful explosion burst forth and shook the earth, the guard in the watchtower must have woken up, and we saw something that made us smile even in the midst of our fear of the warzone noises: with the dark sea behind, the fast-moving stain was a crazy pattern that not even the person who designed the Pink Panther could have made as beautiful, the dark stain of a body with a green light spewing smoke from its hand, one thousand tangled ropes lashed to that body that raced like a one-hundred-metre hurdler, one thousand ropes with imprisoned birds, seven or eight bird-cages tied to its waist, jumping like buoyant balloons, imprisoned birds at his ankles crying out that they didn't want that forced ride of high-speed hopping and skipping across the water and the white surf of the dark sea; in his other arm more tangled ropes of parrots and I don't know what-all other birds, even hens, all a pattern of brilliant green light and the bottom of the sea telling us—now no one could doubt it—that the stain running with bird-cages as it rode over the sea as though it were solid earth, that stain was the body of Sea Foam, laughing at having come down the beach so quickly with creatures hanging from his body as he unachieved the take-off of true-flown flight.

A few terrified voices had already begun to be heard in the distance and, far away from the storage shed, almost as he crossed the garbage dump, Foam had started to slow down, leaping higher. Dona Libânia hugged us again because the explosion was very loud, as though in imitation of a cannon. "Cardinal point south!" 3.14 shouted with a nervous laugh, looking at me, then looking straight ahead. Yes, it could only be the south. A strong light invaded the sky, turning as yellow as fire, and the ground shook; we saw blazes break out in the area around the storage shed, heard the noise of exploding bullets like popcorn forgotten in boiling oil. Dona Libânia trembled. A beautiful fire made a perfect circle around the Mausoleum; the guard from the tower dropped his weapon and fled down the alley behind commando André's house, another very strong outburst that felt like two outbursts hurled cement into the air and made the Mausoleum tremble. "Northwest!" I shouted. The air began to fill with fine dust and the blazes roared higher as though trying to lick the very tip of the rocket; there was fire even on the side where we had not put any whisky, a beautiful symmetrical fire almost drawn with a set of school compasses, and then an even stronger explosion made all of Bishop's Beach tremble. Even those who didn't want to had to come out onto their verandas or onto the street to spy out whether this was, in fact, war, or a mere surprise of colours in the sky about which someone had forgotten to warn the population during the news broadcast on National Radio of Angola. The Mausoleum lighted up all at once, with the brilliant sounds of the dynamite that we had codified with our very cardinal points: huge noises on all sides with lights that seemed to accompany them, and now it wasn't only that yellow fire that can be sparked by bullets or explosives: a mixed light of various colours grew in the middle of the dazzling disorder, with small and large explosions, which did not frighten us as much as before. It was even more beautiful to watch the reflection of the darkness igniting in the sea, which, even though dark, now had on its hide some lights that imitated the strong tones of watercolours, when Sea Foam's green light went out, leaving him standing in the garbage dump almost still and dragged in all directions by the birds, with him laughing out loud, turned into a scarecrow from the fields which in the end became a clown who was everyone's friend and didn't want to frighten anyone.

3.14 released my sweating hand. We had spent the whole time kneeling, concentrating on simultaneously feeling the fear created by the enormous explosion and all the colours entering our open eyes and mouths. Even today I don't know how to explain the fact that we didn't even speak about how our hearts had beaten so fast when we stood up on aching legs, both of us with tears in our moist eyes as we saw, dexploded at night in that way, our beloved Bishop's Beach covered with an ashen dust from the luminous explosion that had finally occurred.

A big explosion awoke other birds in the trees and the fish in the sea. We saw colours from a carnival of fire: yellows, reds pretending to be the colour of oranges in a green that was bluish without being aquamarine, all shining as they imitated stars that knew how to dance in a sky that was no longer dark from being so brightly lit up with our explosion, so beautiful from lingering in the noises and the pretty colours that our eyes looked upon, never to be forgotten in the passage of time—not for our whole lives.

The sky stayed lit up from other explosions almost without sound, a madness of brilliantly coloured patterns that I had never seen in the movies when the cowboys blew up mountains with more dynamite than we had used.

"Maybe there were other materials in the top of the cabinet." 3.14 spoke in a very low voice. "It's possible the other Soviet boxes had other things that shouldn't be mixed with fire."

"Shouldn't be?" I smiled. "Of course they should be. Just look at how beautiful our sea is when it's all aglow!"

Everyone looked at the lighted sky of Bishop's Beach, that sky that gazed down at people who were still coming running from other streets to get to the square and have more space and more darkness to watch the ceiling of the city of Luanda.

People who had gone away came back. The Comrade Gas Jockey came running. From far off, he must have thought that the light of the explosion was one of his gas pumps, that someone had set down a lighted cigarette, or even that the Soviet dynamiting had already started. Others, elders, came to see up close, because from a distance they had thought that it was a fireworks show to commemorate some political date that they had forgotten about, or even something related to the Mausoleum itself; still others had said that the explosions could only be by order of the Comrade President, because fireworks shows that big and beautiful had never been seen in Luanda and had to be authorized by the political bureau of the Party.

Many adults arrived; even people from other neighbourhoods began to come down the long street from the Blue District.

During all this time, Granma Nineteen had stayed on her veranda. Then I saw her talking to Doctor Rafael Knock-Knock, and her face took on a worried expression. Maybe Madalena had told her that we had gone out a long time ago.

I looked up at all of the windows of Granma Nineteen's house, even at the window of Granma Catarina's room: they were all shut to keep the dust out of the house. From five o'clock in the afternoon onwards, we were no longer allowed to open the windows, nor to leave the veranda door wide open. Only after the truck that damped down the dust had gone by, and if no mosquitoes had come in from the bushes, did Granma allow us to open the door a crack so that a cool breeze came in. But I figure Granma Catarina wasn't there.

All of the children of Bishop's Beach who had kites to fly began to arrive, as did the children from the Blue District and from Kinanga and from over by those thatched huts that were built right up against the sea. They all understood that the breath of wind was quickly going to increase in velocity, and that it was a beautiful night to set coloured kites flying where there were still reflections of the light of the fire in the sea, so close and so colourful.

In the midst of the chaos, Sea Foam became more excited. A chaos of people left Foam with a troubled look, and he fled away from the mob, just when we wanted to go and speak to him to know what he had seen from the other side of the storage shed, from which he had emerged with the parrots and other birds tied to his body. But he started to run again, disappearing down the other end of the beach, hauling everything, fowl and hens, cages and little birds, dragging, also, the chirping noises of all those beings which, imprisoned in their cages as they were by being attached to his body, must be dreaming of the moment when they would be able to fly home.

"He must be going to release the birds."

"I never thought there were so many of them."

"I never thought he'd come, too." 3.14 looked in a different direction.

"Who?"

"The Boss General."

He arrived in a different car, alone, coming down the hill very quickly and honking for people to get out of his way, stopped the car near the gas pump, got out with his tunic full of medals that shone almost like the tears in his eyes at his disbelief at the smoke and the ongoing noise of small explosions that greeted him.

"Cannot be...How explode like that?" He glanced at the people, who did not answer him. "Where is Comrade Dimitry, Comrade Bilhardov? What happen to Muzzleum?"

I saw glistening tears fall from his eyes. Maybe another general, more of a general than he, was going to bawl him out the next day or even that very night for not having had advance knowledge of the explosion of the Mausoleum on Bishop's Beach.

"Kildren, every body can help. Must put out fire of Muzzleum." Except that no one stirred. They just stood looking at him. "Must get water of sea. Put out fire of Muzzleum. Beautiful verk of Angolan people to remember President." Now he spoke, now he shouted, as he cried like a child. "Every body get pail, put out fire, save verk of Muzzleum, so much verk of Soviet comrades..."

Many people didn't even know who he was. They looked at him with pity, perhaps thinking that he was one of the diligent labourers who came early every day and left late, who ate the construction site's dust and felt the sun's heat on their heads, because some of them didn't even have helmets: some, the Angolans, lived far away and left the site in the back of a big truck that possibly gave them a ride part of the way home; others, the Soviets, went to sleep full of sad nostalgia for their homeland in the far-away.

"Kildren." He looked at us. "General want to ask question: who know Comrade Bilhardov? Does he hide in dog cage?"

I wasn't going to reply. No one had spoken with him; but 3.14 couldn't keep silent.

"Here in the street we only have parrot cages, Comrade Medalov." 3.14 made the gang laugh.

"Attention, kildren!" The Boss General thought he was talking to his soldiers.

"Get lost, tupariooov, Russkie!"

We shouted in chorus and fled towards the sea, Pi, Charlita and I, in a sprint that imitated the birds. Even with our eyes closed, we still knew the way to the sodden sea.

But we didn't see, in fact we never saw, what continued to occur there near the square. Each of us knows how to tell the story of every moment of that night, each conversation, because we spent many years putting together our versions of events and discovering things that only time brought to light, and in the end magic summoned the coming together of all of the people who had invented that explosion in Angolan colours at the Soviet construction site. We were still running towards the sea and not looking behind us. We didn't know whether the Boss General was pursuing us nor whether Granma Nineteen wanted to call out to us because at last she had seen us, nor whether Granma Catarina was hiding behind the wooden shutters laughing at that night. We didn't count how many parrots flew through the sky without colliding or losing altitude. We didn't hear the noise of the birds that Foam released one by one, cutting their ropes and reciting verses of Cuban poems to give the birds strength, and frightening them with his loud voice, which at times is a way of telling a bird that fear is being close to humans, that they must fly far away to a home far away from the cities and the wars and the children's pellet guns and the Soviets' cages.

We didn't see the fire at the main gate of the Mausoleum catch on the treetops of Dona Libânia's house, and the Boss General shout that it wasn't that fire they had to extinguish, it was another one, the fire on the most important part of the construction site, and the ordinary folk laughing and bringing pails and wash-basins with water from their houses or from the sea, we didn't see the Comrade Gas Jockey hurriedly open the gas pump, connect the little generator to be able to activate the gas pump, set the needle to gasoline, and attach a long hose to the end of his own hose full of salt water

"don't be afraid, get back"

he shouted, and when the fire was about to enter Dona Libânia's house, he engaged the pump and began spraying a salty water that put out the fire in the tall trees in Dona Libânia's yard, even though the gasoline fumes set off some sparks in the branches, which all had the same fire-yellowed colour as they were left damp and limp even after the fire went out

we didn't see the general looking terrified because he had never seen a gas pump put out a fire in old trees, then get into his car because by that time Senhor Tuarles had already said to Dona Isabel

"go upstairs and get the AK-47"

Dona Isabel had even gone already and Senhor Tuarles would have loved to put bullets in the chamber and fire two shots, the general hadn't brought either his pistol or his soldiers and he had to leave

we didn't see Dona Libânia crying with fear and even in that state go and prepare a tea with leftover banana cake that was served on Granma Nineteen's veranda to anybody who wanted it and especially those who had helped to put out the fire, we didn't see it because we were far away, on the other side of the gas pump, on the other side of the square, beyond the sand, beyond the construction site fence, beyond the cardinal points that we had invented, we were over there, stripping off our clothes, laughing, shouting as we called out to Sea Foam, who did not come, readying our bodies to dive, our mouths to smile and our lungs to shout, as we did sometimes beneath the water, laughing in happiness, in those shoutless submerged voices and invented jokes that all could hear, to such an extent for one day someone to have said that those were "blue shouts"

and in this way, with naked bodies feeling a soft breeze, looking at the kites that flew over our square in Bishop's Beach, I, Charlita and Pi, better known as Comrade 3.14, jumped the shells and the holes of the crabs that fled in fear of us, we who sought the experience of the salt water on our bodies, hungry for white surf in the dark sea at that moment of partying and laughter, we were there, in search of where our bodies were able to dance gently on the air in our lungs that had been spared by our shouts, and I remembered the elders who I had met and who sometimes weren't capable of believing in the simple secrets of children, the elders who thought that the cries of the birds were those we heard in the morning or in the late afternoon, when birds are in a hurry to get somewhere and shout for other birds to get out of their way, but those cries, in spite of being shouted, aren't very true, since birds are like children, they need to be beneath the water to give a true shout, it wasn't a child who told me that, it was a bird, Charlita and Pi know it, we all heard the birds shouting beneath the water of the sea of Bishop's Beach, but not that night

at that moment we three were alone in the dark water, diving to shout our blue shouts, and I was thinking: what colour is a bird's shout?, or, as Sea Foam said

"a true shout is only to be imagined or heard by our individual ears, like a true secret, because no one else believes in it"

it was good to feel our bodies, with our skins hot, in the pleasant temperature of the water, turning our heads from time to time to glance and see whether Foam might not be there nearby and wish to bathe with us, "you're crazy," Charlita said, "he only bathes alone, then he stands up to see the fowling stars," and we laughed, how was it that we knew so many of his expressions, "nobody forgets the blinking brilliance of a fowling star," Pi remembered, "fowling stars? never heard of them," Sea Foam used to laugh, "but I've already seen a few of them," we dived as we said these things in the language of blue shouts to see our soaked faces with red, irritated eyes

a last explosion went off at the peak of the Mausoleum and the sky was possessed by a slow gleam

"the world is full of invisible secrets, the sea cools the stars"

I seemed to hear Foam's voice and I stayed with my head poking up out of the water, even though the others were tugging on me to submerge me more, our shouts of half-pretend fear made a tiny noise and we heard the cries of the birds that were leaving for the far-away, we plunged deeper with mouths open, each of us shouting inside the water of the immense sea

"we invented blue shouts"

someone was going to say later, but for me it was a heap of voices imitating the knots of the Old Fisherman's net, shouts all drowned from not succeeding in making any noise other than that poorly realized imitation of the voices of the shells that were close to our ears recounting, without cease, the old secrets that the sea never wanted to tell, and it was on observing the others' laughter, on hearing their blue shouts, that I tried to remember another phrase that Sea Foam had said, but I wasn't able to speak with my mouth full of water and with the words that would not be heard in the ever so salty water of the sea, I raised my neck and peered at the fresh air above, I made signals for them to swim upwards as well and come to hear this other memory, and they came, but a shameful laughter invaded my chest because in the end I had forgotten the phrase again

"what was it?"

they were asking as they looked at my face of someone who had something to say

"let's just go swimming"

I invented, swimming gently like that, the three of us almost touching the bottom with our feet because it wasn't deep here, we were in the pretty area of white sea surf when we saw Sea Foam so close by pretending to be running in a hurry "look at the sky flooded with stars...the stars are the eyes of the shining universe"

he was inventing circles on the seashore with his body, and his dreadlocks hung with shells, and he shouted the exact phrase that I had just remembered and forgotten

"stars whirling in the black desert...I need stars, *compañeros*, I need stars...Because the sky doesn't know how to dance alone!"

Deer Komrad Frend Dona Nhéte,

Forgive Portuguese error. Bilhardov write some letter in hurry to leave, no have time give apersonally Dona Nhéte, your grankildren like destroy so Bilhardov hope letter succeed arrive.

Forgive no goodbye like should, everything sudden, organize with frends from groop sad for land in far-away.

Groop take advantage explozhun of Muzzleum to take plane out. If Komrad General no, all groop prisoner, then organize explozhun in Muzzleum. Bilhardov, your frend, never want participate plan explozhun of houses in Bishop beach. Orders of general for end of verk.

Your family here very booteful. Your grandkildren, your kildren, all very simpatiko and like you very much. Bilhardov speak serious when invite Dona Nhéte come with me to Soviet Union. Snov very booteful in Russia, in my village in far-away. But Bilhardov understand that place is with family.

When you reed these letter I don't know where Bilhardov will be. Maybe can catch all plane to Russia and see family. After Bilhardov write, but they say Angolan mail no verk very gud.

Bilhardov feel miss for Bishop beach and all Komrades, especially Dona Nhéte.

Forgive if explozhun in Muzzleum make problem, but Dona Nhéte family get time and they must start verk again. Bilhardov cover dinamite with sea salt for booteful effect in Luanda sky. The kildren like? One day kildren can rite tell how was Bishop beach after fireverk. Bilhardov no stay see and tell in far-away.

Best vishes, with sadness and respekt, always gud wish for family. Bilhardov no forget conversation with your sister Catarina very funny her mysterious secret only appear when want.

Best vishes to all in Bishop beach.
Bilhardov
Luanda, Bishop beach

Dona Nhéte: pleeze no forget tell your grandsun body of Komrad President Agostinho Neto is gud, away from explozhun. Tell also that alligator in house of Sea Foam is really real. Is Bilhardov who bring food to alligator every thursday. But be careful: alligator grow big...

"Is that what tales from before were like a long time ago?"
"Yes, son."
"So before is a time, Granma?"
"Before is a place."
"A place really far away?"
"A place really deep inside."

GLOSSARY

Spanish Expressions

abuela: grandmother
adiós: goodbye
bailamos: we dance
bailar: dance (verb)
baile: dance (noun)
bienvenido: welcome
buena suerte: good luck
buenas tardes: good afternoon
bueno: good; but also, well
cabrón: bastard
¿cómo?: how? (literal); what? (colloquial)
¿cómo está(s)/ cómo están?: How are you? (singular and plural)
comprendo: I understand
del barco del Chanquete, no nos moverán: ("They won't make us leave old Chanquete's boat"): refrain from a popular song from *Blue Summer* (see below).
desaparecer: disappear
¿dónde está?: Where is?
encantado: Pleased to meet you
errores: errors, mistakes
flores: flowers
hasta mañana: until tomorrow
¿Hay alguien aquí?: Is there anybody here?
hijo de puta: son of a whore
La lluvia no perdona a los que se ponen por debajo de ella: The rain does not forgive those who stand beneath it.
la luna: the moon
La vida es como es: Life is as it is.
mañana: tomorrow
más: more
me gusta: I like
muchacho: boy

muy bien: very good
nada: nothing
el poder: power
planes: plans
poeta: poet
por completo: completely
por favor: please
que te parió: who gave you birth. Understood as part of the insult, "The whore who gave you birth."
sí: yes
todo: all, everything
trabajo: work
tranquilo / tranquila: calm
Yo hablo: I speak
Yo lo sé: I know it

Cultural References

Blue Summer: An influential Spanish television series of the early 1980s, it was widely broadcast in socialist countries. The story revolves around the freewheeling lifestyle of children and adolescents living on a beach.

FAPLA: People's Armed Forces for the Liberation of Angola. The national army of post-independence Angola.

Gabriela: A Brazilian soap opera, popular throughout the Portuguese-speaking world; it is based on the novel *Gabriela, Clove and Cinnamon* by Jorge Amado.

japie: Derogatory term for a white South African.

Kianda: The Goddess of the Sea in Angolan mythology; she has mermaid-like features.

Kimbundu: One of the three major African languages of Angola; spoken in the area around Luanda.

kitaba: A paste made from toasted peanuts.

kizomba: A popular Angolan dance.

Marginal: Broad, scenic waterfront avenue that follows the curve of the bay in front of downtown Luanda.

Odorico Paraguaçu: Comic character on Brazilian television; he is the mayor of a remote town called Sucupira.

ngonguenha: Mixture of cassava root flour with water and sugar.

nyet: No. (Russian)

Pioneers: Socialist organization for children, similar to the Boy Scouts.

quiteta: A type of edible shellfish.

Roque Santeiro: Outlaw character in a famous Brazilian soap opera of the same name; Luanda's largest market was named after this fictitious character.

Sinhozinho Malta: All-powerful landowner in the Brazilian soap opera *Roque Santeiro.*

Sucupira: See Odorico Paraguaça above.

Trinità: Star of Italian spaghetti Westerns.

tuga: Derogatory term for someone from Portugal.

ACKNOWLEDGEMENTS

The translator thanks David Brookshaw and Ondjaki for their help in finalizing the translation.

ABOUT THE AUTHOR

ONDJAKI was born in Luanda, Angola in 1977. He is the author of five novels, three short story collections and various books of poems and stories for children. He has also made a documentary film, *May Cherries Grow*, about his native city. His books have been translated into eight languages and have earned him important literary prizes in Angola, Portugal and Brazil. In 2008 Ondjaki was awarded the Grinzane for Africa Prize in the category of Best Young Writer. In 2012, *The Guardian* named him one of its "Top Five African Writers." In 2013, he was awarded the José Saramago Prize for his novel *Os Transparentes.*

ABOUT THE TRANSLATOR

STEPHEN HENIGHAN's previous translations include Ondjaki's *Good Morning Comrades*. He is the author of a dozen books of fiction, reportage and criticism, including the short story collection *A Grave in the Air* and the essay *A Green Reef: The Impact of Climate Change*. He teaches at the University of Guelph, Ontario.